Praise for *The Man Who Lived Underground*

"*The Man Who Lived Underground* reminds us that any 'greatest writers of the twentieth century' list that doesn't start and end with Richard Wright is laughable. It might very well be Wright's most brilliantly crafted, and ominously foretelling, book." —Kiese Laymon

"Not just Wright's masterwork, but also a milestone in African American literature. . . . *The Man Who Lived Underground* is one of those indispensable works that reminds all its readers that, whether we are in the flow of life or somehow separated from it, above- or belowground, we are all human." —Gene Seymour, CNN.com

"Nothing less than the reestablishing of a major legacy." —*Chicago Tribune*

"A tale for today. . . . [Wright's] restored novel feels wearily descriptive of far too many moments in contemporary America." —*New York Times*

"It's impossible to read Wright's novel without thinking of this twenty-first-century moment. . . . Wright deserves sensitive reconsideration, especially now that so many of us have been proved naïve in our belief that an honest rendering of Black people might lead to recognition of our existence in the universality of humanity." —Imani Perry, *The Atlantic*

"The power and pain of Wright's writing are evident in this wrenching novel. . . . Wright makes the impact of racist policing palpable as the story builds to a gut-punch ending, and the inclusion of his essay 'Memories of My Grandmother' illuminates his inspiration for the book. This nightmarish tale of racist terror re~~~~~~~~~~~~~~~~~~~~~~~~~~~~~~~~~~ *Weekly*

"Propulsive, haunting. . . . The graphic, ~~~~~~~~~~~~~~~~~~~~~~~~~~~~~~~~ ing companion essay that further ex~~~~~~~~~~~~~~~~~~~~~~~~~~~~~~~~~ novel."

"Finally, this devastating inquiry into oppression and delusion, this timeless tour de force, emerges in full the work Wright was most passionate about as he explains in the profoundly illuminating essay 'Memories of My Grandmother,' also published here for the first time. This blazing literary meteor should land in every collection."

—*Booklist* (starred review)

"Like a telegram from midcentury America warning us about our very present, Richard Wright's novel arrived with the shock of recognition for readers in the midst of a reckoning with racial injustice.... *The Man Who Lived Underground* is a masterpiece."   —*Time*

"A welcome literary resurrection that deserves a place alongside Wright's best-known work."   —*Kirkus Reviews* (starred review)

"Never did Wright approach race more directly than in *The Man Who Lived Underground*."   —*Los Angeles Times*

"To read *The Man Who Lived Underground* today ... is to recognize an author who knew his work could be shelved for decades without depreciation. Because this is America. Because police misconduct, to use the genteel 2021 term, is ageless."   —*Chicago Tribune*

"Moves continuously forward with its masterful blend of action and reflection, a kind of philosophy on the run.... Whether or not *The Man Who Lived Underground* is Wright's single finest work, it must be counted among his most significant."   —Clifford Thompson, *Wall Street Journal*

"Enthralling.... You could say that the book's release now is timely, given that it contains an account of police torture.... But that feels false because Wright's story would have been just as relevant if it had been released 10 years ago or 30, 50, or 80—when he composed it.... Maybe, then, it's more accurate to think of *The Man Who Lived Underground* as timeless rather than timely."   —*The New Republic*

"This is a significant work of literary fiction from a legendary author that's absolutely not to be missed."   —*Book Riot*

THE MAN WHO LIVED
UNDERGROUND

The Man
Who Lived
Underground

A Novel

Richard Wright

Afterword by Malcolm Wright

HARPER**PERENNIAL** ● MODERN**CLASSICS**

NEW YORK ● LONDON ● TORONTO ● SYDNEY ● NEW DELHI ● AUCKLAND

Compilation, prefatory note, and note on the texts © 2021 by Literary Classics of the United States, Inc. New York, N.Y. All rights reserved.

A hardcover edition of this book was published in 2021 by Library of America.

THE MAN WHO LIVED UNDERGROUND AND "MEMORIES OF MY GRANDMOTHER." Copyright © 2021 by Julia Wright and Rachel Wright. Afterword © 2021 by Malcolm Wright. All rights reserved. Printed in the United States of America. No part of this book may be used or reproduced in any manner whatsoever without written permission except in the case of brief quotations embodied in critical articles and reviews. For information, address HarperCollins Publishers, 195 Broadway, New York, NY 10007.

HarperCollins books may be purchased for educational, business, or sales promotional use. For information, please email the Special Markets Department at SPsales@harpercollins.com.

FIRST HARPER PERENNIAL MODERN CLASSICS EDITION PUBLISHED 2022.

Interior design and composition by Gopa & Ted2, Inc.

Library of Congress Control Number: 2020941374

ISBN 978-0-06-297148-7 (pbk.)

22 23 24 25 26   LSC   10 9 8 7 6 5 4 3 2 1

Contents

Prefatory Note

SOME READERS may recognize the title of this novel from the short story of the same name in Richard Wright's collection *Eight Men*. Before it was a story, "The Man Who Lived Underground" was the longer work published here for the first time. Recognizing the significance and artistic integrity of the novel as distinct from the merits of the story, the author's elder daughter, Julia Wright, reached out to the editors at Library of America, publisher of the unexpurgated texts of *Native Son* and *Black Boy* (*American Hunger*), to see whether the novel-length version might be published. The publication of *The Man Who Lived Underground*, she indicated, should be accompanied by the essay "Memories of My Grandmother," pointing out that the latter resembled "How Bigger Was Born," written to explain the genesis of *Native Son*, and that it was her father's wish to see the two works published together.

The Man Who Lived Underground was written in an era when lynching and beatings of Black Americans were sufficiently widespread in the United States (not just in the South) to enforce both Jim Crow legislation and unwritten codes of behavior governing interactions between Blacks and whites. Wright's novel captures this environment of fear, just as it reflects anxieties about the events of World War II then unfolding, when the fate of the world seemed to hang in the balance. Those wishing to learn more about how Wright came to create the work that he believed "stemmed more from sheer inspiration" than anything he had written, and about the many influences on its composition, are encouraged to turn to "Memories of My Grandmother" after reading the novel.

The Man
Who Lived
Underground

[Part One]

THE BIG WHITE DOOR closed after him. He pulled his ragged cap low over his eyes, and headed through the summer dusk for the bus line two blocks away. It was Saturday evening; he had just been paid off. A steady breeze from the sea dried his sweaty shirt. Above him red and purple clouds hovered above the edges of apartment buildings. He neared a street intersection, paused, and looked at the slender roll of green bills clutched in his right fist; in the deepening gloom he counted his wages:

"Five, ten, fifteen, sixteen, seventeen . . ."

He walked again, chuckling: Yeah, she never makes a mistake. Tired and happy, he liked the feeling of being paid of a Saturday night; during seven sweltering days he had given his bodily strength in exchange for dollars with which to buy bread and pay rent for the coming week. He would spend tomorrow at church; when he returned to work Monday morning, he would feel renewed. Carefully, so that he would run no risk of losing it, he put the tight wad of crisp bills securely into his right trouser-pocket and his arms swung free. Street lamps blazed suddenly and two lines of lazy yellow gradually converged in the distance before him.

"Mowing that lawn made my hand sore," he said aloud.

Before him was the white face of a policeman peering over the steering wheel of a car; two more white faces watched him from the rear seat. For a seemingly endless moment, in the balmy air of an early summer night, he stood immobile, his blistered palm uplifted, staring straight into the blurred face of a policeman who was pointing a blinding spotlight full into his eyes. He waited for them to question him so that he could give a satisfactory account of himself. After all, he was a member of the White Rock Baptist Church; he was employed by Mr. and Mrs. Wooten, two of the best-known people in all the city.

"Come here, boy."

"Yes, sir," he breathed automatically.

He walked stiffly to the running board of the police car.

"What you doing out here?"

"I work right back there, mister," he answered. His voice was soft, breathless, pleading.

"Who for?"

"Mrs. Wooten, right back there at 5679, sir," he said.

The door of the police car swung open quickly and the man behind the steering wheel stepped out; immediately, as though following in a prearranged signal, the other two policemen stepped out and the three of them advanced and confronted him. They patted his clothing from his head to his feet.

"He's clean, Lawson," one of the policemen said to the one who had driven the car.

"What's your name?" asked the policeman who had been called Lawson.

"Fred Daniels, sir."

"Ever been in trouble before, boy?" Lawson said.

"No, sir."

"Where you think you're going now?"

"I'm going home."

"Where you live?"

"On East Canal, sir."

"Who you live with?"

"My wife."

Lawson turned to the policeman who stood at his right. "We'd better drag 'im in, Johnson."

"But, mister!" he protested in a high whine. "I ain't done nothing . . ."

"All right, now," Lawson said. "Don't get excited."

"My wife's having a baby . . ."

"They all say that. Come on," said the red-headed man who had been called Johnson.

A spasm of outrage surged in him and he snatched backward, hurling himself away from them. Their fingers tightened about his wrists, biting into his flesh; they pushed him toward the car.

"Want to get tough, hunh?"

"No, sir," he said quickly.

"Then get in the car, goddammit!"

He stepped into the car and they shoved him into the seat; two of the policemen sat at either side of him and hooked their arms in his. Lawson got behind the steering wheel. But, strangely, the car did not start. He waited, alert but ready to obey.

"Well, boy," Lawson began in a slow, almost friendly tone, "looks like you're in for it, hunh?"

Lawson's enigmatical voice made hope rise in him.

"Mister, I ain't done nothing," he said. "You can ask Mrs. Wooten back there. She just paid me off and I was on my way home . . ." His words sounded futile and he tried another approach. "Look, mister, I'm a member of the White Rock Baptist Church. If you don't believe me, call up Reverend Davis . . ."

"Got it all figured out, ain't you, boy?"

"No, sir," he said, shaking his head emphatically. "I'm telling the truth . . ."

A series of questions made him hopeful again.

"What's your wife's name?"

"Rachel, sir."

"When is this baby going to be born?"

"Any minute now, sir."

"Who's with your wife?"

"My cousin, Ruby."

"Uh hunh," Lawson said, with slow thoughtfulness.

"I think he'll do, Lawson," said the tall, raw-boned policeman who had not spoken before.

Lawson laughed and started the motor.

"Well, boy, you'll have to come along with us," said Lawson, his manner a strange mixture of compassion and harsh judgment.

"Mister, call Reverend Davis . . . I teach Sunday School for 'im. I sing in the choir and I organized the Glee Club . . ."

"You'd better put the bracelets on 'im, Murphy," Lawson said.

The tall, raw-boned man clicked handcuffs on his wrists.

"Scared, boy?" Murphy asked.

"Yes, sir," he answered, though he had not really understood the question. He had answered because he wanted to please them. Then he corrected himself: "Oh, no, sir."

"Where's your mother and father, boy?" Lawson asked.

"Sir? Oh, yes, sir. They dead . . ."

"Any kin folks in the city?"

"No, sir. Just Cousin Ruby."

"Come on. Let's take 'im in," Lawson said.

His eyes blurred with the first tears he had shed since childhood. The car rolled northward and he noticed that it had grown dark. Yeah, they taking me to the Hartsdale Station, he thought. He had no fear about all this; he looked unseeingly before him, confident that he would eventually give an explanation that would free him. This was a dream, but soon he would awaken and marvel at how real it had seemed. The car swung and turned onto Court Street and sped westward over steel trolley tracks. What would Rachel think when he did not come home on time? She would be worried to death. He was astonished to learn from a big clock in a store window that it was seven. His stomach contracted as he pictured his hot supper waiting for him on the kitchen table. Well, as soon as he identified himself sufficiently at the police station, they would let him go. And later tonight, at home with Rachel, sitting in the easy chair by the radio, he would laugh at this little incident; in telling the story he would hold back the most dramatic parts and make Rachel eager to ask many questions.

The car rumbled on and a ghost of a smile played across his lips. The car's horn sounded and he remembered where he was. Yes, he had to tell these policemen that he was no thug and that Reverend Davis, his friend, was a public figure in the Negro community. He would make the policemen know that they were not dealing with a stray bum who knew nobody, who had no family, friends, or connections....

"That's right, boy. Think up a good alibi," Lawson said.

"No, sir," he exclaimed guiltily. He felt that Lawson's eyes were an X-ray that could look through his skull and read his thoughts. Then he wailed: "Mister, I ain't done nothing. Honest to God, I ain't..."

His voice died as the car yammered over the asphalt. The absurdity of his being carted off to jail made him want to laugh, but he checked himself. He was so confident that he could not take this seriously. So far the policemen had not accused him of anything.

"Say, mister," he began in a high, breaking voice that carried a slight trace of reproach, "what you-all want me for?"

"What did you do with the money?" Lawson countered.

"What money?" he gasped.

"You know what we're talking about, boy," Lawson said in a loud voice. "The money you took after you killed 'em..."

Panic agitated him. His lips moved several times before words came.

"*Killed* who?" he wailed. His voice rushed on without waiting for an answer. "Mister, I ain't *killed* nobody. Why don't you go back and ask Mrs. Wooten . . . ?"

"Mrs. Wooten didn't come home till late today, hunh?" Johnson asked.

"Yes, sir. Like most times I was working there by myself, polishing the car, washing the windows, painting the basement . . ."

"We know all about that," Lawson said.

He had the terrifying feeling that these men knew what he would be doing at any future moment of his life, no matter how long he lived.

"Here, boy, straighten up," Murphy said.

He sat up and Murphy pulled forth the roll of bills and counted them.

"Where's the rest of it?" Murphy asked.

"I ain't got no other money, mister. I swear I ain't!"

As the car streaked forward, Murphy inserted the money into an envelope and put the envelope into his pocket.

"Any bloodstains on 'im?" Lawson asked.

Murphy and Johnson examined every inch of his clothing, inspected his fingers, looked at his shoes, and even probed into his hair.

"Did you change clothes today?" Johnson asked.

"No, sir."

The car pulled into an entrance and came to a sudden halt, throwing him violently forward. Lawson got out of the front seat and slammed the door. Murphy and Johnson dragged him roughly out and pushed him through a crowd of policemen.

"What you got there, Lawson?"

"We're cracking the Peabody job," Lawson said.

"He sing yet?"

"Naw. We got to sweat 'im," Lawson said.

He attempted to twist around and look at the policeman who had asked the questions, but Murphy jerked him forward. He tried hard to read the grim expression on Lawson's face, but he could make nothing of it. They led him up a short flight of wooden stairs and into a dim hallway. They led him up another flight of narrow winding stairs and pushed him into a small, dirty room that had no window. He stood uncertainly, his eyes wandering about the walls. To his left was a single wooden chair. An electric bulb with a wide green shade swung from the ceiling. The room was filled with a musty, stale odor. In one corner he saw a porcelain spittoon full of slimy mucus. Cigarette and cigar stubs littered the floor.

The policemen unlocked the handcuffs and pushed him into the chair. He watched them pull off their coats and caps and hang them on hooks along the walls. They rolled up their shirtsleeves with leisured deliberation, moving about silently. For a long while they neither spoke to him nor looked at him. Then all three of them came and stood in front of him.

Murphy picked at his teeth with the end of a dirty matchstick.

"I ain't done nothing!" he said, looking from face to face.

"Come on. Quit stalling," Lawson said. "Tell us all about it . . ."

"Mister, I swear before God . . ."

Lawson bared his teeth and bent forward quickly and

gave his face a resounding slap with the naked, red palm of his hand. A flash of scarlet zipped past his eyes and his entire body leaped with rebellion. His lips felt frozen and numb; as they thawed, they began to ache and sting and bleed.

"Maybe that'll help you to remember," Lawson said.

"Mister, for real, I ain't done nothing," he mumbled, sobbing.

"What time did you leave Mrs. Wooten's house?" Murphy asked.

"Just a little while before you-all come along in the car and picked me up," he whimpered.

"Boy, you *know* what we mean! We mean *earlier* today!"

"I didn't leave earlier today, mister . . ."

"You *did*! You went next door!"

"No, sir. I didn't go next door."

"Didn't you climb through Mrs. Peabody's window?"

"*No*, sir, mister! I ain't *never* been over there!"

"Didn't you go over to the Peabodys' right after Mr. and Mrs. Wooten left this morning?" Johnson asked.

"No, sir, mister . . ."

Lawson turned to the others.

"He must've gone about ten o'clock. The doctor says they've been dead for nine hours . . ." Lawson turned back to him. "Now, listen, boy, you may as well tell us. You left about ten, didn't you?"

"No, sir! Please, mister . . . I don't know what you talking about . . ."

"What time did Mr. Wooten leave the house this morning?"

"A little before nine, sir."

"And what time did Mrs. Wooten leave?"

"About nine-thirty, sir."

"Nobody was in the house with you after nine-thirty?"

"No, sir. I was there by myself. But I didn't leave."

"You're a cool one, aren't you, boy?" Lawson asked.

"No, sir, mister."

"You stayed right there in Mrs. Wooten's house when we were in the Peabody home? You saw us investigating, didn't you?"

"*No*, sir, mister! *No*, sir . . ."

Lawson struck him across the mouth. He cupped his face in his hands and leaned forward, moaning and sobbing. Johnson leaned over him, yelled in his ear.

"What did you use, boy? A hatchet?"

"I ain't never killed nobody. *Nobody* . . . I swear, you-all got me wrong, mister."

Murphy reached above his head and clicked on the electric light and the bright glow shone directly into his eyes. He blinked, his bloody lips hanging open.

"Well, boy," Lawson said in a low, somber tone, "we're going to keep you right here until you tell us what you did . . ."

"Mister, I tell you I ain't done nothing," he cried, his mouth twisted, tears streaming down his black, wet cheeks.

"All right," Lawson said. "It's up to you. If that's the way you want it, then that's the way you can have it. Now, just sit there and catch hell . . ."

He stared at Lawson, trying desperately to understand what was happening to him. He was dreaming; yes, that was it, and Lawson was a dream and he was demanding that he do something impossible.

"Which one did you kill first?" Lawson asked.

He leaped to his feet and screamed with all the air of his lungs, "I ain't killed nobody!"

Johnson pushed him back into the chair.

"Take it easy, boy."

"You killed Mr. Peabody first so you could have your way with his wife, didn't you?" Lawson asked quietly.

Horror came into his eyes as he clasped his hands and knotted his fingers; his head wagged aimlessly, as though it had become too heavy for his neck. Every limb on his body shook; sober reason told him to say no, but every muscle in his body urged him to say yes and get free of this nightmare.

"I ain't never killed nobody," he said through chattering teeth.

"Where did you hide the money?" Lawson asked.

Curiously, he felt these questions had the power of projecting him into a strange orbit where, though he was not guilty of a crime, they made him feel somehow guilty. He fought against this enveloping mood.

"Mister, I ain't got no money," he spoke in a slurred run of words. "Please, call up Reverend Davis . . ."

"To hell with your goddamn Reverend Davis! We'll make you forget that goddamn preacher yet!" Lawson yelled.

"Please, you-all . . ."

"Answer the questions! When did you kill those two people!"

"Mister, I ain't done nothing to nobody . . ."

Johnson caught hold of his chair and pulled it into the center of the room, then all three of them resumed their pacing in front of him.

"Please, mister . . ." he begged, leaning forward in the chair, blinking his eyes to keep tears from blurring his vision. "Let me send word to my wife . . . She don't know where I am . . ."

"Naw. Let her worry. If you got sense enough to talk, then you can see her," Lawson said.

"I don't know nothing about what you say, mister. I swear to God, I don't."

"You got it all fixed up, ain't you, boy?" Lawson asked.

Murphy walked with seeming aimlessness to the back of his chair, and though he saw him he paid him no attention; then, suddenly, he felt himself being tumbled violently upon the floor as the chair was snatched from under him.

"Just a little sample, boy," a harsh voice came into his ears. "Get up!"

"Yes, sir," he whispered.

He stood and the chair was shoved toward him.

"Sit down."

He sat and they continued their walking, their rubber heels making hollow sounds on the wooden floor, like a drum echoing inside his head.

"Mister, please," he cried, "I don't know nothing . . ."

"Shut up!"

"Please, mister . . ."

"Maybe he's playing out," Murphy said. "Maybe he wants a drink of water . . ."

He saw the three policemen exchange quick glances.

"Sure, sure," Lawson said placatingly. "The boy's thirsty." Lawson came to him and placed a hand upon his shoulder. "Say, boy, how'd you like a drink of water, a cool drink . . ."

He did not answer.

"Talk, goddammit!" Lawson shouted. "We don't give a damn if you sit there and roast! But if you want water, then say so . . ."

"Yes, sir," he whispered.

Though his throat felt as dry as a red-hot oven, he really did not want water; he wanted to go home. Murphy left the room and Lawson and Johnson leaned against the wall and lit cigarettes. Sweat stood on their foreheads and their eyes held a preoccupied look that made him think that maybe he was not really there in the room with them at all, that all of this was some weird dream that must end soon. The door opened and Murphy came in with a glass of water in his hands.

"Here you are, boy," Murphy said, coming forward. "See, we're nice to you, ain't we? We're your friends. We don't want to hurt you. But you got to talk, see?"

"But I done told you all I know, mister . . ."

"Here," Murphy said kindly, extending the glass, "take a drink first . . ."

He reached for the glass and held it timidly in his fingers; ice tinkled against the sides of the tumbler and the chill of the water was soothing to his palm. Lawson and Johnson edged closer. The warm air of the room made the glass sweat and slowly his glands responded to the look of the cool fluid.

"Go ahead and drink, boy. I've got to take that glass back," Murphy said.

He lifted the glass to his lips.

"Wait, boy," Murphy boomed at him. "Tell us what you did with the money you took out of the desk in the Peabody home."

"Honest, mister, I was never in that place in my life . . ."

"Aw, let 'im drink, Murphy," Lawson said.

"Go ahead and drink, boy," Murphy said, seeming to relent, taking a short step backward.

He filled his dry mouth with cold water and was in the act of swallowing when he saw a white fist sweeping toward him; it struck him squarely in the stomach at the very moment he had swallowed the water and his diaphragm heaved involuntarily and the water shot upward through his chest and gushed forth at his nostrils, leaving streaks of pain in its wake. At the same instant the glass leaped from his fingers and bounded with a ringing twang into a corner. Coughing, he pitched prone on the floor, face first, and lay twitching. Pain balled in his stomach and he began to gag amid his coughing as more water trickled through his nostrils and lips.

"Perfect!" Lawson said. "I heard the water squish!"

"I timed it to a split second," Murphy said with a quiet, modest smile.

"You're getting damn good, Murphy," Johnson said.

Trembling, he rose and they pushed the chair forward. Grey and blue eyes continued to regard him with quizzical contempt. He lowered his head in surrender and sighed through open lips. The fit of coughing had made him thirsty and he licked his lips and was grateful for the few drops of moisture he tasted there. He lifted his hand and rubbed his mouth and when he brought his fingers away he found that it had not been water he had tasted, but the tangy salt of his own blood. What they doing to me? he asked himself in despair.

"How long were you working for Mrs. Wooten, boy?" Lawson asked.

"'Bout a y-y-year, sir," he panted.

"How'd you get the job?"

"The ch-ch-church sent m-m-me," he spoke in gasps. "Mrs. Wooten c-c-called Reverend Davis . . . He always s-s-sends us out on j-jobs . . . Reverend Davis g-g-got an employm-m-ment office at the ch-church . . . If you c-c-call up Reverend Davis . . ."

"Quit telling us what to do!" Lawson barked.

He sat crying, his lips slobbering. Sweat trickled from his face onto his hands.

"All right," Lawson said. "If you want to sit here all night, then it's up to you. If you talk, you can get some rest . . ."

"I ain't got nothing to s-s-say, mister," he gulped. "I just want to go home to my wife . . . You-all got the wrong man . . ."

"Johnson," Lawson called, "string 'im up and see how he acts."

"Okay," Johnson said.

Johnson advanced with handcuffs and clapped them about his wrists.

"Come on, boy," Johnson said. "Maybe your brains are in your feet; if they are, we'll get 'em back into your skull."

Johnson yanked him up and clapped steel bands upon his

ankles; then Johnson and Murphy lifted him bodily and swung him upside-down and hoisted his feet to a steel hook on the wall. The steel bands on his ankles were looped over the hook and he hung toward the floor, head first. Blood pounded in his temples and his heart and lungs sagged heavily in his chest. He could barely breathe.

"Well, how do you feel, boy?" Lawson asked.

He could not answer. His sight dimmed. The room went round and round. He swallowed several times. Circles of fire blazed about his ankles and his eyeballs strained against their sockets. Nausea welled up in him and he tightened his throat to keep from retching.

"Mister," he whispered.

"Talk, you black bastard!"

The room and the voices gradually receded. Though his eyes were wide open, he could see nothing. His breath came in heavy heaves and he could feel his body, like a huge pendulum, swaying in space with each throb of his heart. Fire traveled down from his ankles to the calves of his legs, then to his knees; fire finally enveloped his entire body and a great cloud of darkness entered his brain. The next thing he knew he was sitting on the floor and someone was slapping his face.

"Wake up, you bastard!" Lawson was shouting at him.

His eyes opened and his head drooped to one side; his temples pulsed with pain. A heavy weight seemed to be pressing on top of his head. He was aware of a warm trickle of blood seeping down one corner of his mouth and, as out of a dense mass of steam, he heard the distant clang of a fire wagon.

Foolishly, he wondered where the fire was. Then Rachel suddenly filled his mind. Rachel.... He grew frantic.

"I want to go home! I want to go home!" he cried over and over.

"You're going to stay here until you talk, see?" Lawson said. "Get up and sit in that chair."

He rose slowly and would have fallen had not Murphy caught his arm. He sat uncertainly in the chair and his body jerked imperceptibly with each beat of his heart.

"How old are you, boy?"

The voice had reached him from an unknown location and he gazed up aimlessly.

"Twenty-nine," he said vaguely.

"Just twenty-nine goddamn too many years around here, hunh?"

"No, sir."

"Say 'Yes, sir,' goddammit!"

"Yes, sir," he mumbled without tone or spirit.

"Before we get through with you, you sonofabitching nigger, we're going to teach you something..."

Back and forth they walked in front of him. Their white faces were grim and bent toward the floor. The smoke from their burning cigarettes stung his eyes.

"Tell us the truth, boy. You'd been watching Mr. and Mrs. Peabody for a long time, hadn't you?" Lawson asked.

"No, sir," he mumbled.

"Couldn't you see into their bedroom window from the kitchen door where we saw you cleaning this morning?"

"I don't know, mister," he whispered.

"You're a goddamn *liar*! When *we* were in Mrs. Peabody's house we could see *you* . . ."

"I never wanted to look over there, mister . . ."

"After you killed 'em," Lawson's voice went on, ignoring his feeble, protesting answers, "you deliberately went about your work all day as though nothing had happened, didn't you?"

"I don't know what happened over there, mister," he sobbed.

"You're just about the coolest nigger killer I ever talked to," Lawson said. "You're playing a game, but we'll break you, even if we have to kill you!"

They resumed their walking in front of him, their shoes still making hollow thuds on the wooden floor. Each of the men was more than six feet tall and seemed to weigh well over two hundred pounds; their sheer height and weight frightened him, for he weighed but one hundred thirty and stood but five feet seven inches. The room was stiflingly hot; it seemed that he could not get enough air into his lungs and he breathed with short, panting breaths. Encasing his body was a film of sticky sweat.

Time dragged as though by some force outside of himself; the horror of the three men walking in front of him faded and he saw Rachel lying upon the cheap, brass bed he had bought when they had married and started housekeeping nearly a year ago. In his imagination he saw her lying there in the heat of the night, fanning herself, fretful, restless, moving her swollen body about on the bedcovers, sighing, waiting for him. . . . Good God! He had to get home or send word to her *somehow*!

If only they would call Reverend Davis! Or Mrs. Wooten!
Appealingly he looked up at them out of his mood; they still
marched in front of him. He grew hysterical as he felt that he
did not exist for them.

"Please," he whimpered.

"Why did you kill 'em?" Lawson asked, stopping before
him.

He did not answer; the three policemen gathered about
him and questions came tumbling one after the other.

"Where is the hatchet? You used a hatchet, didn't you?
What did you do with the money you took from the desk? Did
you hide it? Did anybody help you with the murder? Come,
nigger, talk! Didn't you plan to rape Mrs. Peabody? When the
mailman rang the doorbell at eleven o'clock, he scared you
off the woman, didn't he? When you were through, you went
back to work at Mrs. Wooten's, didn't you? You thought nobody's ever going to think you did it, didn't you?"

"I don't know what you-all talking about," he groaned in
desperation and despair.

Lawson grabbed the collar of his shirt and snatched him
forward; again he lay sprawled on the floor. He smelt the
acrid odor of a cigar butt. Blows came so hard and fast that
the sheer pain of them made him realize that they were beating him with a blackjack. He groaned. The toe of a shoe came
like a jabbing hot iron into the nape of his neck; he gave a
short, involuntary scream. They jerked him to his feet and
pushed him again into the chair. He saw a blob of blood on
his shirt.

"Do you want to talk now, boy, or do you want some more?"

His lips moved, but no words came. Johnson placed a hand tenderly upon his shoulder.

"Listen, boy, don't you want to go and see your wife?"

"Yes, sir," he managed to whisper.

"Then tell us what you did."

"I . . . I-I ain't done n-n-nothing . . ."

A fist exploded between his eyes and he went backwards, toppling with the chair; his head struck the wall, banging twice from the force of the blow. Semidarkness seized him and it seemed that he was lying atop a fast moving streetcar, watching many blue sparks of electricity shower down plume-like as contact was made with the high-tensioned trolley wire overhead. The world veered from left to right. Then he was a little boy stealing a ride on the tail end of a speeding truck. . . .

II

Hours later he felt cold water drench his face; with a quick start, he was wide awake. They propped him in the chair and his vision cleared. He saw that there were four men in the room now: Besides Lawson, Johnson, and Murphy, there was a man in a grey business suit. He held a white piece of paper in his hand and leaned toward him.

"I've got something here I want you to sign, boy," the man said. "I'm the District Attorney. Now, listen, I don't want these men to keep bothering you, see? So just sign your name . . ."

Again habit made him try to answer, but he could form no words.

"Don't you want to see your wife, boy?" the man in the grey suit asked.

He did not answer; Rachel seemed unimportant now. He wanted sleep and an end to his pain.

"The D.A. asked you do you want to see your wife, boy?" Lawson shouted into his ear.

"Yes, sir," he mumbled, dreamily.

"Look, then," the grey suit said in a caressing voice, "sign this paper. I wrote it all out for you. Just sign it and you can see your wife . . ."

He stared with unblinking eyes at a white sheet of paper covered with blurred lines of black.

"What does this paper say?" the grey suit asked.

He tried desperately to read the paper, but he could not focus his eyes. As he sat staring at the white blur, he heard the faint clatter of horse hooves on the pavement below, then the jangling of metal against metal. *My God! That's the milkman. . . . It's four o'clock in the morning. . . .*

"Let me go home," he moaned.

"Sign the paper and you can go," the grey suit said.

His eyes filled with tears. His head ached and the voices of the men came out of a dream, repeating: "*Read the paper and sign it . . .*" The grey suit shoved the paper into his fingers and he held it for a moment, looking at the print running in hazy black waves across the wavering white. Then the paper fluttered from his numbed fingers and slid along the floor.

"Sonofabitch," Lawson muttered and slapped him again.

He fell from the chair and his body rolled along the floor until it struck a wall; he lay inert, wrapped in semidarkness.

A wave of heat engulfed him and in a confused dream he thought that he was back at Mrs. Wooten's house, running the electric lawn mower over the bright green grass. Then rough fingers tugged at his clothes and he was lifted back into the chair.

"Sign the paper, boy!" he heard Lawson shouting.

He wanted to answer, but he had no control over his numbed lips. The faint clang of a streetcar came to him from far away. Lord, what time is it? He sagged toward the floor, but the stinging blows of their bare palms against his cheeks kept him hovering precariously within the circle of consciousness. The white splotch of paper waved again before his eyes.

"Sign it and get it over with," the grey suit said.

He swayed and groaned. Times without number the thunderous voices cut into his ears and his brain and his blood. But he made no attempt either to read or sign the paper. He felt hypnotized, in the grip of a force stronger than he. There were periods of utter blankness when he was not aware of what was being said. He sat uncertainly on the edge of the chair, his lids blinking now and then to shut out the intense glare of the electric light that dangled before his eyes.

Hot tears searched their way down his black cheeks; he swallowed and leaned forward, yearning for oblivion, yet telling himself that he had to sign the paper. The smear of white fascinated him with a deep and terrible finality. He tried to focus his eyes again, but he could not. The harsh voices began again: "*Sign the paper, boy . . .*"

"Yes, sir," he mumbled, more to himself than to them. Then, for the first time, he began to weep, copiously, without restraint. "Yes, sir . . . Yes, sir . . . I'm going to sign it . . . I'm going to sign it . . ."

The grey suit stood in front of him and he felt a smooth oblong object in his fingers; it was a fountain pen.

"Just sign your name and we'll take you home . . ."

Yes, all he had to do was write his name and they would take him home, home to Rachel. . . . Home, he thought, with rising and hysterical hope. Elation seized him; truly, he felt nothing important could come from his signing his name to that splash of white that danced before his eyes. Yes, only good could come from it, something different from this torture. He held the fountain pen in shaking fingers as Lawson brought the paper close to his eyes. There was a book under the paper.

"See, boy," the grey suit told him, "we're putting this book under the paper so you can write. Now, steady yourself . . ."

"Yes, sir," he breathed.

But he did not move; he just held the pen and looked at the paper through bleary, red-rimmed eyes. They shook him until his teeth rattled.

"Sign it!"

Oh, yes; he had to sign this paper, had to write his name, and then they would take him home. He put the pen to the paper and tried to write; a pain shot from his shoulder to his elbow and the line of ink trailed downward foolishly, in a wild scrawl.

"Here, let me help you," the grey suit said soothingly.

"Yes, sir . . ."

Slowly, he scribbled his name, with the arms of the grey suit holding him, partly guiding him. When he was through, he still held the pen over the island of white, poised, as though willing and ready to write on and on. The grey suit took the pen and paper away.

"Can you read it?" Lawson asked.

"Yeah, I think it'll do," the District Attorney said, holding the paper at arm's length and squinting at it.

"Look," Murphy said. "Here's his signature on his Selective Service Card. Do they look enough alike to get by?"

The District Attorney compared the two pieces of paper.

"Yeah," the District Attorney said reflectively. "It's good enough."

"Well, we got this much," Johnson said with a tired sigh, putting on his coat.

"What're we going to do with 'im?" Murphy asked.

"Did you book 'im yet?" the District Attorney asked.

"Not yet," Lawson said.

"Then you'd better book 'im and put 'im on ice," the District Attorney said, handing the paper to Lawson. "Hang on to the confession for the inquest."

"Okay," Lawson said, folding the paper and putting it carefully into his pocket. He crossed over and got his cap and coat. "Say, maybe we ought to take 'im to the Peabody home . . ."

"Oh, all right. I don't think he'll react much," the District Attorney said.

"Say, maybe we ought to take 'im to see his wife," Johnson put in eagerly.

"Yeah," Lawson agreed. "Nobody can say we weren't good to 'im if we take 'im back to his wife for a few minutes, eh?"

"He won't be able to sit in that chair," the District Attorney said. "You'd better put 'im on the floor."

The chair was jerked from under him and again he lay prone with closed eyes. He heard footsteps going away and then he could hear no more. He drifted into a faraway land of blinding sunshine, filled with huge white-hot rocks. He was tramping with bare feet over burning sand, sweating profusely, winding his way among a vast stretch of white-hot rocks. His throat was constricted from thirst, but there was no water, only glaring sunshine and sizzling sand. He noticed that each of the huge white-hot rocks had a white piece of paper tied to it and there was a black fountain pen in his right hand. From glowing rock to glowing rock he went and signed his name to each tag of white paper, signed his name carefully and slowly, whispering: "*Yes, sir . . . Yes, sir . . .*"

III

When he opened his eyes, he saw the three policemen looming above him. A bitter taste clogged his mouth.

"He's pooped out," one said.

"Funny, he could hardly sign his name on that confession, but when we booked 'im, he wrote all right, didn't he?"

"Yeah. They do crazy things when you sweat 'im."

"How you reckon he is?"

"Oh, he's all right."

Propped on his feet between two of the policemen, he slithered to the door, his head lolling, his arms dangling askew.

They led him into the hallway and then down steps. When he was in the driveway of the police station, the fresh air and sunshine stimulated him; but before he could get his bearings, he was pushed into the rear seat of the car. Lawson got behind the steering wheel; Murphy and Johnson sat at either side of him. The motor roared and the car backed into the street, turned, and went forward over gleaming trolley tracks.

Lingering pains ached in his body. His nostrils were full of the odor of stale sweat on his clothes. Full consciousness returned to him and he tensed his muscles against an array of invisible dangers, asking himself: Where they taking me? I want to go home. . . .

"Mister, can't I go home now?" he asked in a childlike plaintive whine.

"You'll go home soon enough," Lawson said.

Vaguely, he remembered that he had signed his name to a paper, but that did not seem important. If only he could get away from these policemen, everything would be all right. As the car zoomed on, he looked out at the streets and discovered that he was nearing Mrs. Wooten's. Maybe they had decided to ask Mrs. Wooten who he was? *Good!* Everything's going to be all right, he told himself. Yes, there was Mrs. Wooten's big white house! He was almost at the end of this nightmare! Then his heart sank as he recalled that Mrs. Wooten was not at home. . . . Why had he not thought of that before? What was wrong with him? When Mrs. Wooten had paid him off, she had told him that she and Mr. Wooten were leaving for the country for the weekend. So nothing would be settled here after all; he might as well tell the policemen that. Just as he leaned forward to speak, the car pulled to a stop in front of the Peabodys' home.

"Remember this house, boy?" Lawson asked casually.

"Yes, sir," he answered. "It belongs to Mr. Peabody. But I don't work here, mister. I work next door and they ain't home yet . . ."

"We know all about that," Lawson said in a voice whose tone indicated that he had access to a vast knowledge.

They pulled him out of the car and led him up the steps.

"This is Mr. Peabody's house," he protested.

"You mean it *was* Mr. Peabody's house," Johnson said.

He was brought to the front door and he stood with Murphy and Johnson holding his arms. Well, Mr. or Mrs. Peabody would surely tell these men that he had never been in their house, and that would settle this thing once and for always. But no one rang the bell; instead, they watched him.

"There's the bell," he told them, pointing.

Lawson laughed softly.

"You're certainly the coldest goddamn black sonofabitching raping nigger killer I ever laid eyes on," Murphy said. "You know damn well nobody can answer that bell. There's no one there . . ."

"I didn't know nobody was there," he mumbled in confusion, doubting his own logic, skeptical of the real world that hovered before his eyes.

"You *do* know it!" Lawson snarled. "You *killed* 'em!"

Stupidly, he stared at them; then an irresistible smile broke on his lips. Out here in this sunshine, amid these normal and familiar sounds, it was impossible that these men were seriously accusing him of murder.

"Mister, I wouldn't do a thing like that," he said in a voice that betokened that he was talking confidentially to a close and trusted friend.

"I'll be damned," Lawson said. "Murphy, unlock the door."

Murphy took a key from his pocket and inserted it in the lock and turned it and swung the door open.

"Step in, boy," Lawson said.

He hesitated, looking into their faces.

"Get the hell in!" Lawson said, giving him a shove.

He stumbled through and stood apprehensively in a dim hallway. What were they going to do with him? They had accused him of having killed Mr. and Mrs. Peabody, but surely they did not really mean that. He had not been in this house in his life. Yes, Mr. and Mrs. Peabody would come out of some room at any moment now and tell them that they were wildly wrong, and then he would wake up out of this mad dream.

"All right, take 'im upstairs," Lawson said.

Lawson led the way; Murphy and Johnson caught his arms and he walked up the stairs between them. At the top of the steps they paused.

"All right," Lawson said impatiently, "what in hell are you waiting for? Take 'im on in."

"Okay," Johnson said.

He was led to a door, which Murphy flung open; he expected a voice to sound imperiously, demanding that this be stopped. He stood in the doorway, his lips open, blinking his eyes at a deluge of golden light. The array of images that caught his eyes was of such a nature that he stood for a full minute without really knowing what he saw. Then he recoiled, his breath whistling through his teeth, his knees bending to leap. Some protective part of his mind kept his eyes from believing what he saw, kept the meaning of the strange images from registering in his consciousness. The room looked as if some hurricane had swept through it, wrecking everything. There was evidence of a gory, mortal struggle. The bed was piled high with tumbled, white sheets that showed red stains. The curtains had been ripped from the windows and lay in stringy strips on the floor. On the green wall near the bed were many blobs of red spatter. The drawers of two chests were pulled out at different distances and clothing was half-spilled. A small desk lay smashed. A table was overturned. The mirror of a vanity was shattered and splinters of glass glinted in all directions. A grey rug held viscid pools of dark liquid.

"Naw," he whispered.

"Get on into the room," Lawson said, shoving him again.

He stumbled forward, then drew back. Lawson gripped his arms and held him. The horrible sight smote him at close range and his knees gave. He attempted to wrench his arm free, but Lawson clutched him tightly. The blood-spattered room, lit to glaring distinctness in the sunlight, made his head throb.

"Come on, boy. Show us what you did!" Lawson said.

Johnson caught hold of his coat and tried to pull him to the center of the room; he gave a wild jerk and before the policemen knew what was happening, he had hurled himself through the doorway and into the hall.

"Stop, boy!" Lawson shouted.

Murphy sprinted after him and flung his weight against him and bore him to the wall.

"Hold 'im!" Lawson yelled.

Panting, he looked at Lawson, who had drawn and leveled a gun at him.

"That was a dangerous thing to do, running that way," Lawson said with sober quietness.

Johnson led him back into the room. Over and over they asked him to tell what he had done, to show how he had done it. Several times he tried to open his lips to speak, but his jaws seemed locked. Finally, he made no attempt to speak at all; he merely shook his head when they talked to him. As he stood there gazing about in fear, the full seriousness of his predicament became plain. If he were being accused of a crime as horrible as this, then he was in deep danger. He quailed inwardly as he remembered that he had actually signed a paper without having read it! He should have known better than that. Perhaps he had only dreamed he had signed a paper. Yet, he *must* have signed it, for this bloody room was proof that he had committed himself in some way. Oh, God! But he had been tired to the point of death when he signed it; then they ought not hold him responsible. How could he get out of this? He clenched his fists in a maddening frenzy of helplessness; he held himself in this attitude until his muscles ached, then he relaxed, surrendering to fatigue. He wanted to fall to the floor right now and sleep until he had his strength back, until he was fresh and keen again; and then he would be able to cope with this horrible thing, would be able to clear himself of this blood and this accusation of guilt. Nothing seemed to come plain to him as he stood there, everything was foggy, gummy, blurred. He whirled and faced Lawson, his lips moving silently; finally his words broke forth.

"Please, mister . . . I don't know nothing about all this . . . You-all got me wrong!"

His right hand waved itself weakly through the air, as though to sweep the room of its crushing sense of condemnation from sight. The eyes of the policemen were upon him steadily.

"Come on, boy, make it easy for yourself," Lawson told him. "Remember, you've already signed a confession. You've already admitted your guilt . . ."

All strength left his body and he dropped to the floor, sobbing helplessly, trying to talk in long, drawn-out whimpers. He lay on his face and Murphy stooped and rolled him over on his back; he closed his eyes to shut out the bright sunshine. His mouth was twisted in a tortured line.

"What you-all doing to me?" he cried.

"Get up and talk," Lawson muttered, kicking him gently, as though some strange quality of compassion had suddenly entered him.

The blow did not hurt, but he almost stopped weeping as he wondered why Lawson had kicked so *lightly*. . . . A crazy impulse to burst into a prolonged laugh seized him and it was with difficulty that he suppressed it. Why had not Lawson kicked him hard? Yes, as the question came to him, he felt that he knew the answer; it was that what these men said, what he said, the blows and curse words, were all neutral and powerless to alter the feeling that, though he had done nothing wrong, he was condemned, lost, inescapably guilty of some nameless deed.

"All right, get 'im up," Lawson said.

They lifted him and took him from the room; but even when he was in the hallway, he could still see the room, the wave of sunshine pouring through the windows and splashing the red-spotted sheets on the bed, glinting on the innumerable shards of glass scattered about the grey rug among the dark blotches of blood; he still saw the battered desk, the overturned table, the protruding drawers of the chests, the wine-red splotches on the green walls. . . . He gagged as he tried to speak.

"I . . . s-s-wear b-b-before . . . God, I-I . . . ain't d-d-done nothing . . . I h-h-hope to . . . d-d-die if I ain't . . . telling you the t-t-truth . . ."

"Don't worry," Lawson said with a quiet, assured smile, "you'll die all right . . ."

He stared at Lawson; at once, as the words had fallen from Lawson's lips, all feelings of anger and protest fled. He found himself smiling at Lawson and nodding his head in agreement.

"Yes, sir," he found himself saying, "We'll all die. But I didn't do this . . ."

"Don't get sassy," Lawson snarled.

"Come on," Murphy said, jerking his arm.

They led him down the stairs. His feet stumbled; if they had not held on to him, he would have plunged headlong down the entire length of steps. He stood in the hallway as the police-men spoke among themselves in low voices.

"We taking 'im back to the cooler?"

"Say, I thought we were going to let 'im see his wife?"

"That's an idea."

"No one can say we mistreated him if we let 'im see his old lady, hunh?"

They looked at him with musing tolerance.

"Say, boy, where do you live?" Lawson asked.

"Sir?"

"Come on. Where do you live?"

"Oh, yes, sir. I live at 49 East Canal Street. Yes, sir," he said, nodding his head vigorously like a child anxious to be believed.

"All right," Lawson said. "Let's go."

They led him down the steps and along the walk to the wait-ing car. Again he was in the back seat, sitting between Murphy and Johnson. The motor throbbed and the car moved swiftly through Temple Street. Without looking he knew that the sidewalks were filled with black people, people like himself, but he did not want to think of them; at some time during the recent past they had become alien to him. The reality of Rev-erend Davis had fallen from him; the reality of Mr. and Mrs. Wooten had faded. He was claimed by some strange, powerful reality which the policemen represented, but he felt that the mere sight of Rachel would launch him again into the normal routine of his living. All he felt and knew right now was that the car in which he sat was carrying him toward home, to the familiar walls; and, once home, he would come back alive. The car picked up speed and sailed onto Market Street and swung west to State Street where they paused for a red light. When the green light flashed, the car traveled along State Street, northward, to Canal Street and swung eastward and pulled to a stop directly in front of his door. *He was home!* His body was poised for action. But nothing happened; minutes passed. What were they waiting on?

"Mister," he ventured timidly, "this is my place. I live here. My wife is up there . . ."

The policemen did not reply. Perhaps his voice had not been heard? Perhaps he had only imagined that he had spoken? Is this a dream? he asked himself.

"Yes, sir," he began. "I live here . . ."

"We know that," Lawson said. "You just sit still and keep your damn shirt on." Lawson turned to Murphy. "You want to take 'im up?"

"Okay. I'll take 'im," Murphy said, shrugging.

"We'll wait here for you," Lawson said. "Give 'im ten minutes with her. That'll do."

"Okay."

"Think you can handle 'im all right?" Lawson asked.

"Oh sure," Murphy said. "He'll be no trouble, not after last night . . . He's like a baby." Murphy turned to him. "Ain't you, boy?"

"Yes, sir," he said, nodding; he had not really heard the question.

The car door was opened and Murphy caught his arm and led him across the sidewalk and into the vestibule. Murphy paused.

"Got your key?"

"Sir?"

"Your key, goddammit!"

"Yes, sir. Yes, sir."

He pulled a key from his pocket. Murphy took it and opened the door and led him into the dim-lit hallway.

"Now, listen here. Be quiet when you go up these steps, if you don't want another slap, you hear?"

"Yes, sir," he answered eagerly.

"What floor you live on?"

"Second, sir."

"All right. Go on, in front."

He walked on, eagerly, pacing himself so that Murphy would not prod him. He paused in front of his two-room apartment.

"This it?" Murphy asked.

"Yes, sir."

Murphy inserted the key in the lock and turned it and opened the door and pushed him noiselessly inside. Everything was quiet. Where was Rachel?

"That you, Freddie?"

His heart leaped for joy at the sound of Rachel's voice. Yes, this nightmare was ending! He stood rooted, fearing to answer lest he destroy his newfound freedom that hovered above him, this freedom that was about to descend and reclaim him. The words burst from him.

"It's me, honey!"

He tried to run to her, but Murphy's fingers bit into his arms.

"Take it easy," Murphy whispered fiercely.

He walked down the hall toward the bedroom; the door was half ajar and he stood looking at it, afraid to push it open. Was this real?

"Freddie! That you?" he heard Rachel calling again and there was rising hysteria in her voice.

He opened the door and saw Rachel lying upon the bed, her swollen body shaking with weeping.

"Where you been? I'm all by myself . . . Look at your *face*!" she exclaimed. "Lord, what happened to you?"

He ran to the bed and caught her in his arms and stroked her hands and then buried his face in her hair.

"Aw, Rachel," he mumbled.

"What happened to you, honey?"

His arms tightened about her as he felt her body stiffen.

"Who's that man?" she asked in a tense whisper.

He had almost forgotten Murphy; he wanted to turn his head and look at the man who was plaguing him, but he could not.

"Don't mind him," he heard himself telling her insistently. "That's all right. I'm here now. Everything will be fine." He lifted his head and looked at her brightly, as though trying by sheer force of mental effort to create trust and stability in a world gone awry. "Miss me?" he asked. When she did not answer, he laughed hysterically, then he had to choke back his sobs.

"*Who is that man?*" Rachel wailed in despair. "*What happened?*"

"Honey, forget him. It's all right, I tell you. Everything's going to be fine . . ."

He heard Murphy's heavy footsteps come into the room and he turned his head and forced himself to glare defiantly at him. Murphy laughed softly.

"Go right ahead, boy, and don't mind me," Murphy said, with a small, knowing laugh. He took a seat and crossed his legs and looked quizzically around the room. For a moment he seemed bored, then he lit a cigarette and settled back to wait with an expression of inexhaustible patience.

"What happened to you? *Who* is that man?" Rachel demanded.

He felt her soft fingers fumbling about his face. He did not answer her; he had not really heard her. His consciousness was possessed by the man who waited behind his back. Convulsively he caught her and held her close, as though this was his last chance to be with her. Suddenly he stood up from the bed and gazed wistfully down at her swollen body; then propelled by a sense of outrage, he whirled and confronted Murphy with glaring eyes full of hate. Murphy gazed back at him with a quiet, steady, secret smile.

"Why don't you leave me alone? I want to stay with my wife," he shouted.

"You made a bargain with us, remember?" Murphy chided him pointedly.

Anger surged in him and for one glad moment he felt that he was coming fully awake, that he was shaking off this terror, wiping away the cobwebs that clogged his brain.

"Go 'way!" he screamed.

"What's wrong, Freddie?" Rachel cried out from the bed. "*Talk* to me . . ."

"It's all right," he mumbled in bewilderment.

"Well, boy," Murphy announced, rising. "Let's get going."

"Naw, naw, naw, na-a-aw!" Rachel screamed as her body gave a wild lunge.

"He's got to come with me," Murphy said in a quiet, fateful tone.

For a magical moment he was in complete possession of himself. He stepped confidently toward Murphy to denounce him, to tell him that he had no authority to compel him to do anything. Then Rachel screamed and he turned quickly back to the bed. Her scream was so distressing that even Murphy started involuntarily.

"Freddie," Rachel panted after she had regained her breath, "it's happening . . ."

"What?" he asked.

"The . . . b-b-baby . . . Get me to the hospital . . ."

"That's all right," Murphy said. "Just wrap her up, boy, and get her down to the car. We'll take her."

"Yes, sir," he mumbled with a crestfallen air.

Childlike, he bent and wrapped the quilt around Rachel; she groaned and doubled her fists. He lifted her and she huddled tightly against him.

"Come on, boy," Murphy said, holding the door open.

He stumbled into the hallway with Rachel in his arms. Weakness made him teeter toward the wall.

"Be careful, boy," Murphy cautioned him.

"Ain't you coming with me, Freddie?" Rachel whimpered. "Lord, what's the matter? You won't talk to me!"

He walked the length of the hall and his body grew wet with

sweat. He kept on down the stairs and when he reached the vestibule his knees felt like water. Murphy held the outer door for him. With half-closed eyes, he swayed in the middle of the sidewalk with Rachel in his arms.

"Where you-all taking me?" Rachel asked distrustfully.

"To the hospital," Murphy told her.

Lawson and Johnson had got out of the car and stared.

"What in the world is this?" Lawson asked incredulously.

"She's having a baby," Murphy said in disgust. "Good Lord, could I help it?" There was a moment of astonished silence. "We got to take her to a hospital."

"Put her in the car," Lawson said resignedly.

He lifted Rachel into the back seat and held her on his lap. Rachel groaned. The car doors slammed. Johnson and Murphy crowded into the back seat with him. The car plowed through traffic to Main Street and dashed southward, the siren sounding sharp and thin in the sunlit air. It did not seem that he was holding Rachel in his arms; it did not seem that she was going to have a baby. Invisible hands seemed to be pressing some alien destiny upon him. The car reached Ocean Parkway with the siren screaming a prolonged blast. Traffic stopped. Lawson pivoted the car onto Oak Street and stopped it at the curb, in front of a hospital.

"Here you are, boy," Lawson said.

He was scarcely aware that the machine had stopped. The siren died and he heard Rachel sobbing.

"I'm in pain," she whimpered.

"Come on, boy," Lawson called.

The car door was opened and he staggered to the sidewalk,

sagging under the heavy burden of Rachel. She was still whimpering, her muscles tightening spasmodically.

"You'd better take that woman, Murphy, or he'll keel over with her," Lawson said.

"Okay," Murphy said. "Let her go, boy."

He felt Murphy taking Rachel from his arms. Panic seized him.

"Naw," he said, clutching his wife fiercely.

"Turn her loose, or I'll clip you one," Murphy said.

He loosened his arms about Rachel; Murphy held her now. He felt lost; as long as he had held her in his arms, he had felt that there was the barest chance that he might elude this shroud of mist that surrounded him. But with Rachel gone, he was lost. . . .

"Think you can handle 'im up there, Murphy?" Lawson asked.

"Sure," Murphy said. "He's like a trained puppy. Come on, boy, walk in front of me . . ."

"Yes, sir," he whispered.

He led the way uncertainly across the sidewalk. Someone opened a door and he stepped into a shadowy hallway filled with the strong scent of disinfectant. Several white-coated attendants came forward. There was a whir of many voices, but he did not understand what was being said.

"And who is he?" he heard a woman ask.

"Her husband," Murphy said. "He's in my custody."

"You mean he's under arrest?" the woman shrilled.

"We won't discuss that, lady," Murphy said.

"This way," the woman said.

The next thing he knew he was standing in an elevator, being lifted violently upward. He roused himself and saw Rachel in the arms of Murphy. Two black women dressed in white were looking intently into Rachel's face and mumbling something to her. He tried to listen, but he could not rouse himself sufficiently.

He took an aimless step through the door and found himself in a brightly lit corridor. The nurses followed Murphy out.

"You may put her down, now," one of the nurses said.

Carefully, Murphy stood Rachel on her feet and the two nurses took hold of her arms and led her forward through swinging doors.

"Boy," Murphy said with a tight smile, "you make a lot of trouble, don't you?"

"No, sir," he said, abashed with a sense of guilt.

"Sit down," Murphy said, pointing.

He slid limply upon a bench and Murphy sat beside him. He felt a vague panic which he could not understand, as though something extraordinary was about to happen to him. He looked around. Men and women walked about casually. His tension eased.

"Here: a cigarette." Murphy offered his pack.

Timidly, he took a cigarette and held it unconsciously in his fingers and did not think to ask for a match or to search for one in his pockets. He saw a yellow flame dancing before his eyes and he drew back in fright.

"What in hell's wrong with you?"

"Nothing," he whispered.

But he did not reach for the light. Murphy squinted at him.

"Here, hold your cigarette," he said.

"Yes, sir."

He reached forward and held the cigarette to the flame, but he did not put it in his mouth as he did so.

"What the hell!" Murphy exclaimed. "You can't light that cigarette that way."

"Oh," he said.

He discovered his mistake and put the cigarette between his lips and puffed vigorously as though it were already lit.

"Goddammit, are you crazy?" Murphy asked.

His hand froze in midair. Quickly he leaned forward with the cigarette between his lips and touched it to the flame and inhaled twice, then he held the cigarette tightly between his fingers. A wave of sleepiness came over him and he did not remember the cigarette until its fire burned him. The cigarette dropped to the floor.

"I'll be damned," Murphy said.

His body stiffened; a white blur was standing in front of him. He looked up and saw a nurse.

"She's in birth now," the nurse said.

"Yes, ma'am," he whispered without understanding what her words meant.

Murphy flicked his cigarette away and rose and walked to and fro in the corridor, looking now and then at him. With some remote part of his mind he was aware of Murphy, but that sharp focus of attention with which he had always lived from day to day was not functioning now. Murphy came up and stood directly in front of him.

"Hey, boy, wake up," Murphy said loudly. "What're you doing? Sleeping with your eyes open?"

"Yes, sir," he mumbled dreamily; then added quickly: "Oh, no, sir."

As he spoke he did not even lift his head; Murphy's voice seemed to have come from far away. The black shine on Murphy's shoes contrasted sharply with the stony whiteness of the tile. Then he saw Murphy's shoes going away, leaving their blurred image before his eyes. He looked up and saw Murphy go to the door of the men's room, pause, glance back over his shoulder, as though to reassure himself that he would remain sitting there, then go from sight. At last he was alone; at last that constant threat of nameless punishment was gone from him, for a little while. An impulse, not a thought, but just a vague gathering of all the forces of his body urged him to escape, to run off while there was time.

He rose and looked about. At the far end of the hall he saw a nurse mount a stairway with a loaded tray. He went to the stairway and stood looking at the descending steps, then started down, leisurely, deliberately. Yeah, I signed that paper. . . . He went down four flights and found himself in a corridor near an open window. He looked out, then stepped away. Lawson and Johnson sat in the police car below him in the street. He went down the hall to another window through which he saw a black, cinder-paved courtyard about ten feet below him. He glanced around; no one was in sight. Yeah, I ought to jump. . . . He landed on his back and his head hit the pavement. A sheet of white flicked past his eyes and for a moment he was completely out, though his eyes were open and gazing directly into the sun. He came to himself and looked down. Hanging like a shimmering curtain before him was a vast smudge of pink that gradually turned into a blob of lemon; the lemon resolved itself into a dab of green that grew smaller and finally converted itself into a smeary mesh of violet that vanished. He could see clearly now.

He pulled to his feet and saw to his right a driveway leading out of the hospital yard. To his left stood an ambulance whose metal surface glinted in the sun. From his rear came a tinkle of glass; he turned and, through an open door, saw a back boy washing dishes in the hospital kitchen. The fragrant odor of cooking had been in the air all along, but he had excluded it from his mind; now he was dizzy with the desire to eat. His legs wobbled with indecision; he heard the distant clang of a streetcar and he jerked nervously to attention.

I got to get out of here. . . . He walked unsteadily down to the iron gate and down the sidewalk, persuaded in his sense of direction only by the fact that he knew that he must get away from the police car. But, once he was on the street, he promptly forgot that he was fleeing and he ambled aimlessly with his eyes on the pavement, foolishly counting the concrete squares as he passed them; he lost count, then his eyes carefully followed the middle line of the sidewalk. He caught a glimpse of someone passing and he lifted his eyes and looked ahead of him quickly and guiltily, like a child surprised in an act of mischief. The next moment he was laughing quite without reason.

He was sweating excessively and he noticed that the air was growing close and humid and the sky was rapidly clouding. It was a minute before he realized what was happening; rain was falling, cold rain that made him shiver. He ran a few steps and jerked open the first door he encountered and found himself in a small vestibule. The chill of the rain roused him and he ran his fingers gingerly over the rough surface of the smudged walls of the vestibule, then gazed through the glass of the door out at the falling rain lashing up and down the darkened street. A stab came to his consciousness: A siren, faint at first and then rising sharply and drawing nearer, sounded from the direction of the hospital.

He held his breath. Swishing through the slanting rain was the police car in which he had ridden. Yeah, they looking for me. . . . He laughed quietly, feeling safe, secure. The siren died plaintively in the distance. He had to do something; but what? He felt in his hip pocket and got cigarettes and matches; he smoked in silence.

Through the glass of the door a movement caught his eye; thin columns of water snaked into the air from the tiny perforations in a manhole cover. The gushing columns stopped suddenly, as though the perforations had become clogged; then he saw the lid of the manhole lift slowly a foot into the air as a grey spout of turgid water snaked up from the underground. For a moment the water juggled the circular cover, then let it fall to the pavement with a loud bang. He was fascinated, waiting for the manhole cover to be tossed up again.

"Pardon me, please."

He whirled and a tall black man was staring at him.

The man caught hold of the doorknob, then paused.

"You live in this building?"

His lips parted and he nodded slowly.

"Oh, you're the new tenant on the third floor?"

"Yes, sir," he whispered.

"Dunbar is my name," the man said.

He stared, then extended his damp hand; the man gazed at him intently.

"You look like you're all in. Did you move in today?"

"Sir? Yes, sir."

The man laughed, then stepped to the sidewalk. Was the man suspicious of him? Would he encounter the police and tell them that a stranger was lurking in the vestibule? He eased open the door and followed the man until he disappeared. He stepped back into the vestibule and gazed about with an air of annoyance. Then he shook his head, laughing.

He smoked in chain-fashion and the vestibule was thick with blue clouds. When he looked into the street again he was astonished to see that the rain had stopped and that the air was growing rapidly lighter. The siren sounded again and the police car sped past, going back toward the hospital this time. The water that had flooded the sidewalks was flowing back into the gutters. The manhole cover exposed a crescent that gaped in the pavement like a black slip of moon. From behind a pile of grey clouds the sun emptied cascades of yellow into his eyes. He blinked. A car careened near; there was a loud screech of brakes as it stopped suddenly to avoid the man-hole. He laughed. The water in the gutters had now gone into the water-drains and irregular patches of sidewalk were dry. Then, suddenly, the sun was swallowed once more by cloud-masses. The wind rose and a steady downpour beat a muffled hum. The siren sounded again somewhere nearby, then died. He waited, tense. This time the thirsty scream came from the distance. He wished he were a tiny insect that could crawl into one of those crevices in the brick wall; he would be safe then. People would pass him as they went about their daily business.

Hungrily the siren whined close by and he saw the police car whip down the street; he watched it disappear in the pall of tumbling rain. Yes, they were searching the streets for him now, weaving in and out of each block. I got to get out of here, he thought. Quickly, he hatched a tentative plan: He would wait here in this vestibule until he heard the siren sound again, and, if it came from far off, he would creep out and go—where? He did not know. But he had to leave; to remain meant risking capture and a renewal of torture. He lit another cigarette and puffed. Then the siren gave him the signal he was waiting for; its shriek came from far off and, as it sounded, it grew fainter, telling him that the car was going away from him. He opened the door and stepped into the rain and the cool, damp, fresh air. He took a few random steps, then stopped and looked curiously at the gaping manhole, half expecting to see the sewer water leap up again and toss the cover about. For some unaccountable reason—acting like a child filled with an unappeasable curiosity—he crossed the sidewalk and stepped over the gutter in which a torrent of water swirled and walked unsteadily to the center of the street and stood over the half-opened manhole. No water was gushing from it now; he stooped and squinted down into it, but could see nothing. The droning roar of water sounded in the black depths of the underground. He glanced up guiltily. Then he was stiff with terror; the siren was coming closer. It was so near that he had a wild idea that he had been dreaming and had not heard the approach of the siren and had suddenly awakened and now it was almost upon him. Frantically, he glared about. Should he run back into the vestibule? Would he have time? Instinctively, he bent over and peered again into the dark manhole, not with just casual curiosity this time, but stimulated by urgent impulse. The siren drew nearer and beat upon his tired ears. He looked up and down the street, but the police car was not in sight. Perhaps it was coming around a corner? So vividly did he imagine that it was just around the corner that he had a momentary hallucination: *He saw the car bearing swiftly down upon him.* . . . He blinked his eyes; there was no car. A tremor of relief went through his body and he dropped to his knees and his hands reached for the curved rim of the manhole cover. The siren hooted its warning and, with a gasp of physical strength, he jerked the cover far enough off the manhole to admit his body. Resting the weight of his body on both of his arms, with his fingers clutching at the rim of the manhole, he swung his legs quickly over the opening and lowered himself quickly into the rustling, watery blackness of the underground.

IV

He hung an eternal moment by his fingertips; then he felt rough prongs and he knew at once that sewer workmen used them to lower themselves into manholes. Fist over fist, he let his body sink lower; finally he could find no more steel prongs and he swayed in black space, listening to the siren that seemed to be howling at him from the very rim of the manhole. He dropped into water that was surprisingly warm and was washed violently forward into a vast ocean. Frenziedly his fingers clawed the water, seeking some solid object to grasp. His body was whirled round and round; while spinning in the water, he gave up. His head struck the concrete wall of the sewer and he wondered if he would be battered to death. He flayed his arms wildly and his fingers sank into a slight crevice. He reached upward with both hands and managed to steady himself by pressing the flat palms of his hands hard against an invisible wall. Instinctively he measured the strength of the current and stood slowly, bracing himself against the tug of water to balance himself. The water came up to his knees and dashed past him with fearful velocity.

The siren hooted directly above his head, deafening him; then he heard a prolonged screech of brakes. The siren song died. He stood with his muscles flexed against the rushing water and looked upward through the manhole. Yes; they had found him; they would see that open manhole and would look down upon him in just a moment. He held his breath and gritted his teeth; looming above him in the rain was Lawson's white face. He heard Lawson say: *How did this damn cover get off . . . ?* He saw the steel cover moving slowly and then it clanged into place. He was still; the upper world was shut from sight and its sounds were muffled. The whispering rush of the water now droned louder, creating an illusion of another world with other values and other laws. With aching chest, he stood knee-deep in the pulsing current, breathing heavily in utter darkness, filling his lungs with the sharp smell of warm, yeasty rot. But even here in the underground, above the droning rush of water, he was amazed to hear again the faint blare of the siren, penetrating with needle-point sharpness into the hot, close air of the sewer.

Gradually his breathing subsided and his taut muscles relaxed. Even though he stood knee-deep in hostile water, even though his entire body was drenched in what seemed to him a cloud of hot vapor, even though his throat gagged at the reeking odors, he felt that he was safe for the first time in many long and weary hours, felt that he was at last beyond the reach of the three men who had tortured him and extracted an outrageous confession of guilt from him, had made him accept the responsibility of a crime of which he knew nothing. He sighed and looked up and saw that the manhole cover had several small holes through which many delicate fingers of hazy violet light were falling and weaving a mottled pattern of shimmering magic on the surface of the streaking current.

He stiffened as a car swept past along the wet pavement overhead, its heavy rumbling soon dying out, like the sound of a gigantic plane winging its way through a dense, wet cloud. He had never thought that cars could sound like that; everything seemed so strange and unreal under here. He did not know how long he stood there in the darkness, knee-deep in flowing water, musing over the sound of the car.

[Part Two]

THE ODOR of fresh rot had become so general that he no longer had the sensation of smelling it. He found his cigarettes, but discovered that his matches were wet; he searched further and came across a folder of matches in the pocket of his shirt and managed to strike one. It flared weirdly in the wet gloom, glowing greenishly, turning red, orange, yellow. He lit a crumpled cigarette and puffed; then, holding the flame above his head, he searched for something to hold on to so that he would not have to keep his muscles flexed against the pouring current. His eyes gradually adjusted themselves and he saw that the sewer was about five feet wide and some six feet high and the color of the steaming walls was murky green.

To either side of him two slimy brick walls rose and curved above his head to form a dripping, mouse-colored dome. The brick upon which he stood was fashioned to create a wide, sloping V-trough through which the grey water washed. To the left the circular tunnel vanished in ashen fog. To the right was a sudden down-curve into which the water plunged. He knew now that had he not regained his feet so soon, he would have been swept to his death into that watery pit, or if he had gone down into any other manhole he probably would have drowned. Above the heavy rush of the current he heard sharper juttings; several smaller streams were being fed into the sewer, spewing from smaller conduits.

The match flame died to a faint glow, then went out. He struck another and saw a mass of debris sweep past him and clog the down-curve; the water began to rise rapidly and he wondered if he could climb out before it drowned him. There was a prolonged hiss and the debris was sucked from sight; the current lowered again. He understood now what had made the sewer water surge up and lift the manhole cover; the down-curve had become temporarily obstructed. . . .

He was in danger; he might slide into a down-curve; he might wander into a pocket of odorless gas and become asphyxiated; or he might contract some horrible disease. . . . He should leave, but an irrational notion made him remain. To his left the convex ceiling sloped to a height of less than five feet; he stood debating, wanting to walk to where the ceiling swooped low so that he could hold on to it, and at the same time wanting to climb out and take his chances.

With cigarette protruding from flexed lips, he watched the slate-colored water break in creamy foam where the current struck his knees; his curiosity was overcoming his fear. He wanted to know what lay at the end of these mist-shrouded labyrinths, to feel more of this mood that threw everything into such a peculiar light. He waded with taut muscles, his feet slipping over the slimy bottom, his shoes sinking into spongy slop. He reached the lowered ceiling and pressed his left palm against it; he struck another match and his eyes widened. Nestling in a niche of the curving wall was a long metal pole. Yes, some sewer workman had left it. He reached for the pole and a quick whisper of scurrying life flicked past him.

He held the match closer and saw a huge rat, wet and coated with slime, blinking beady eyes and showing tiny fangs. The rat scrambled frantically to the brink of the narrow ledge, its forepaws clawing for a hold on the slick brick. The light blinds 'im. . . . The rat lifted its pointed head and waved its nose about. He lifted the rod slowly, then let it fly with swift motion; he felt the impact of the rod against the rat's soft body and in the same instant there came to his ears a shrill piping. The grizzly body splashed into the dun-colored water and was snatched out of sight, spinning in the scuttling stream.

He waded forward, into the narrowing cavern, using the pole to sound the depth of the water. He struck another match; high up near the ceiling of the sewer, amid loose brick, was a hole with walls of earth leading into blackness; a small pipe ran through it. The hole drew him like a magnet. The flame wavered out. He struck another match and poked the rod gingerly into the hole. It was dry; the sewer water had not reached it. He decided to explore it. A returning sense of the life he had once lived aboveground restrained him, making him feel that this whole experience was outlandish. Why crawl into that hole? He justified himself by whispering: I won't stay long in it. I'll crawl in and see what's there and come out. . . .

He pushed the rod before him, pulled himself upward, got to his hands and knees, thrust his head forward and crawled. After a few yards he paused and struck another match. Ahead was darkness. He crawled on, reaching out his hand at intervals to feel the way. He paused again, struck by the strange silence. It was as though he had traveled a million miles away from the life of the world. Lured by the darkness, he crept forward and the sides of the dirt tunnel grew narrower and, as he inched ahead, he could sense the bottom of the tunnel lowering slightly. He tried to feel the dirt ceiling, but could not. He rose and stood straight up; there was no ceiling within touching distance. Though he had but a few more matches, he risked striking one; the black tunnel went on. He walked a long way and then stopped again, curious, afraid. Where was he going? He scratched another match to flame and peered ahead; the passageway led on into the same monotonous darkness. The match went out. Then, as he put his right foot downward, he found that it swung out into open space. He drew back in horror. What's this? he asked aloud. He poked the rod forward and it almost slipped from his fingers as it dangled into emptiness. He stood listening and straining his eyes, but he could see and hear nothing. Sweat broke over his body as he imagined the earth caving in upon him and burying him alive. . . . Quickly he struck another match and looked; the dirt floor sheered away steeply. Holding the flaming match as high above his head as he could, he leaned outward and forward, peering; yes, he could see dry dirt some five feet below him and the passageway in which he stood seemed to widen beyond into a small cave. He looked upward and saw a rough, concrete ceiling. Was he in some space beneath a basement? He stiffened; he heard a feathery cadence that he could not identify. The match ceased to burn.

Using the pole as a makeshift ladder, he slid down along it until his feet touched the ground and he stood apprehensively in darkness. The air smelt fresh and he could still hear faint sounds. He poked about cautiously, his hands before him, his ears still catching sounds, his fingertips searching space for solid surfaces. Suddenly he felt a brick wall. He followed it and the strange sounds—which he had ignored for a little while—became louder. Again he stopped and strained his ears. *What was that?* The vast overhanging silence made what little sound that did trickle through seem odd beyond description. Yet, those strange sounds were somehow very familiar to him; that was it: *strange* but *familiar*! It was as though he were trying to remember something almost erased from his memory. Was it music he was hearing? Or perhaps singing? Or was it a trolley crashing past over steel tracks? Or a siren? Or perhaps a baby crying . . . ?

He went forward, walking carefully over the dirt so that his footsteps would not drown out the faint sounds. The farther he went into blackness, the plainer the sounds became. He pushed on; the sounds were coming to him loudly now. Yes, *singing*! That was it! He stopped and listened with open mouth. Where was it coming from? He felt that he was a little boy hearing a band playing around the corner; yes, he had to run and hear that singing. Then the identity of the singing burst upon him; it was a church service! The singing was so near that he could feel the timbre and pitch of the voices, yet the darkness made it seem as though the voices were coming from within some enclosed crater of the moon. Entranced, he groped on and the waves of melody rose.

Jesus, take me to your blessed home above
And wrap me in the bosom of thy love . . .

The singing was on the other side of the brick wall. That's a colored folks' church down in one of them sunken basements. . . . Excited, he wanted to observe the church service without being seen, without being a part of it. His fingers combed the brick wall for an opening, no matter how slight. He was frantic, possessed. He looked to the left, to the right, down to the blackness of the ground, and then upward and was startled to see a bright sliver of light some seven feet above him falling obliquely into the darkness, cutting the air like the long sharp blade of a razor. If I can look through that crack, I can watch 'em. . . . He struck one of his two remaining matches and held the flame above his head and saw several rusty pipes running along the length of the dingy ceiling. Standing on tiptoe with the dying match in his hand, he photographically located in his mind the exact position of the pipes. The match flame sank and he sprang upward; his hands clutched a pipe. He swung his legs to and fro and tossed his body onto the bed of pipes. There was a slight creak and he thought that the whole tier was about to crash; but nothing happened. He edged to the crevice and saw a narrow segment of black men and women, dressed in black robes, singing, holding tattered song books in their black palms. His first impulse was to give vent to a loud laugh, but the laugh choked in his throat. Then he wanted to leap through the quarter-inch of crack, straight into the midst of those foolish people and gather all of them about him, telling them: "Don't *do* this to yourselves!"

His emotions subsided and he came to himself. What was he saying? A sense of the life he had left aboveground crushed him with a sense of guilt. Would not God strike him dead for having such thoughts? As he lay upon the bed of pipes, he knew this: His life had somehow snapped in two. But how? When he had sung and prayed with his brothers and sisters in church, he had always felt what they felt; but here in the underground, distantly sundered from them, he saw a defenseless nakedness in their lives that made him disown them. A physical distance had come between them and had conferred upon him a terrifying knowledge. He felt that these people should stand silent, unrepentant, with simple manly pride, and yield no quarter in whimpering. He wanted them to assume a heroic attitude even though *he himself* had run away from *his* tormentors, even though he had begged *his* accusers to believe in *his* innocence.

His arms grew numb; he swung his legs down, one at a time, and dropped lightly to the dirt floor. Pain throbbed in his calves and a deeper pain, a pain induced by the naked sight of the groveling spectacle of those black people whose hearts were hungry for tenderness, whose lives were full of fear and loneliness, whose hands were reaching outward into a cold, vast darkness for something that was not there, something that could never be there, churned within him. *Good God!* Then he mused in the darkness. Yeah, there's something that makes folks say *God.* . . . He shook his head in bewilderment.

He had to get away from this. How long had he been down here underground? He did not know; in this darkness time stood still for him; it seemed that the only sense he had of time was when a match flared and the burning flame measured time by its fleeting duration. Plotting his sense of direction, he groped through the black shadows toward the hole leading to the sewer and the waves of song subsided. The rod was as he had left it, leaning against the wall. He took it and climbed back into the hole and started over the familiar ground, feeling the dirt flooring ascending as he went forward. Finally, he caught the faint sound of flowing water and it made him conscious of the measurement of time. So engrossed was he in his feelings of relief at finding his way back that he bumped his head again; he had reached that point in the passageway where the ceiling swooped low. He dropped to his knees and began to crawl. Now that he felt relatively safe, weakness engulfed him. He came to where the earth ended and he heard the noise of the current.

Since he had last crawled out of that water, his feet had become almost dry and now he was loath to wet them again. The water made less rustling in its flowing; no doubt the rain had slackened and most of the water in the sewers had run to the sea. Ain't no use in staying here, he thought. He climbed out and stood up to his ankles in sewer water and looked around. Ought he to go up into the streets? What would he face if he lifted that manhole cover? At the mere thought of it he became tense; yes, then indeed he would stay. But what could he do down here? As he stared about in the dimness of the sewer, tiny prongs of hazy gold spilled suddenly from the manhole cover and played magically upon the surface of the flowing current. Yeah, them's street lamps, he mused. Must be night now . . . How was Rachel? He pictured her as being at home, then remembered that he had left her at the hospital. More and more he found it repugnant to think of her, as though the image of her crowded more important things from his mind.

He took a step forward, then stopped, frozen, his eyes riveted. What's that . . . ? A strangely familiar object beckoned and repelled him. He went closer and squinted. Then he exclaimed, "Aw . . ." Lit by the light sifting through the manhole cover was a little nude brown baby snagged by debris and half-submerged in water. At first he thought that the baby was alive and he moved impulsively forward to save it, but his roused feelings told him that the thing was dead, cold, nothing, the same kind of nothingness he had felt while looking through the slit at the men and women singing in the church. Water streaked about the tiny head, the tiny body, the tiny arms, the tiny legs, cracking in white foam and rushing onward. He felt the muscles of his body contracting unconsciously as he looked at the shriveled limbs. The tiny eyes were closed tightly, as though in sleep; the tiny fists were doubled, as though in vain protest; and the tiny mouth gaped black as though in an eternal and soundless cry.

He straightened and drew in his breath. Some woman's thrown her baby away. . . . He felt as though he had been standing for all eternity looking at the tan skin lit with ghostly light, white foam blossoming about the head as cascades of veined water skimmed impersonally about it. He flushed with a nameless shame and involuntarily took a step backwards and his lips moved in an effort to utter angry words against the whole configuration of the senseless world. This thing was his enemy; it condemned him as effectively as had those policemen. It made him feel guilty. But, at the same time, he felt that his guilt was futile, for what could he do in the face of this?

He lifted his hand to sweep away this obscene vision, but the knowledge of his helplessness made his arm fall listlessly to his side. Then he acted; he reached forward with his right foot, and, as he reached, he closed his eyes so as not to see when his wet shoe touched the dead flesh; he felt his shoe push the baby's stiff body from where it had been lodged. He kept his eyes closed for a long time, imagining that he saw the little baby twisting in the current as it washed from sight. He opened his eyes and stared into the misty cavern into which the baby had vanished, then he placed his knuckles in his eye sockets, listening to the water as it rushed past in the somber shadows.

II

He sloshed on down the sewer, poking the rod before him, his feet squishing slimy objects. At times he would sense a sudden increase in the tug of the current as he passed some conduit whose grey waters were swelling the stream that shot past his feet. A few minutes later he saw ahead of him another patch of light sifting down from a manhole cover; he was nearing another street intersection and there came to him a chorus of noises that gradually grew to a deafening rumble. Yeah, cars and trucks. . . . He stood directly under the manhole cover and looked down to his left; a stagnant pool of sludge covered with a grey-green scum was lit to distinctness by the falling columns of light. At intervals the scum would swell and a balloon-pocket would rise slowly and spherically, filling with gaseous air, glistening with a greenish sheen, and then burst with a hissing sound. Ten seconds later another dilation would rise and burst. Then another. He shook his head to break the spell. He could stand no more. He turned and tramped back to the dirt cave by the church.

Back in the cave, he stumbled over an iron pipe about four feet long. He went to a brick wall, sat upon the ground and began digging with the pipe. Don't want to make no noise. . . . He dug until he became thirsty. Well, there was no water; there was nothing to do but kill time or go aboveground. The bricks were coming out easily now. He took out another brick and felt a soft draft blowing into his face. Excited, he listened for sounds. There were none. He made the hole large and crawled through into a dark room and collided with a wall. He went to his right, feeling his way. The wall ended and his fingers toyed experimentally in space, like the antennae of an insect.

His body tensed. He heard a human voice, faint and far off. He went forward into the darkness and his feet struck something that sounded hollow, like wood. What's this? He felt with his fingers. Steps . . . Where did they lead? Should he go up? Stooping, he pulled off both his shoes and mounted the steps cautiously and saw a chink of yellow light showing through a keyhole. The voice came clear; a man was speaking. He placed his eye to the lock and at first he could not make out what he saw; directly in the narrow line of his vision was the nude, waxen body of a black man stretched out upon a long white table. The invisible voice droned on in indistinguishable words, neither rising nor falling. About the black, naked figure—with its wax-like and semi-transparent pallor—were many medical instruments. Upon a green wall was suspended a huge glass container filled with a deep red liquid. He craned his neck, still puzzled; then he was shocked to see the tip end of a black object lined with pink satin. A coffin. . . . This is an undertaker's place. . . . He shuddered and a fine-spun lace, icy and invisible, covered the skin of his body.

Suddenly he heard a throaty chuckle sound in the yellow room. He sighed audibly; it seemed that he had been crouching before the keyhole for an endless time. Halfway down the steps it occurred to him that there should be a light switch nearby; he tiptoed back up and felt along the wall and found an electric button. He fingered it for a long time, wondering whether to turn it on. An impulse of recklessness made him flick the knob and a blinding glare smote his pupils so hard that he was completely sightless. If someone opened the door, he would be defenseless against an invisible foe. . . . His pupils finally contracted and he wrinkled his nostrils at a peculiar smell which he had been subconsciously aware of for a long time. Some kind of stuff they use to embalm. . . . He went down the steps and looked about. There were piles of lumber, several coffins, and a long work bench. In one corner he saw a tool box. Yeah . . . that would come in handy; he could tunnel through walls with them. He went to the box and lifted the lid; there were nails, a saw, a hammer, a crowbar, a screwdriver, a bit, a brace and planes. He looked for a flashlight, but there was none. He did find, however, a light bulb, a socket, and a long length of electric wire.

Memorizing the location of everything, he tiptoed back up the steps and switched off the light; he held still a moment, listening. The voice beyond the door droned on, talking, laughing easily, lazily, sensually. He went back down the steps and pulled on his shoes. He lifted the tool chest and carted it to the hole. Would the noise of the falling box make someone come down and investigate? But he had to have those tools! He lifted the box and shoved hard and the box hit the other side of the wall with a loud clatter, then all was quiet. He waited, listening; nothing happened. Head first, he crawled through and stood in the dark cave. He grinned; the tense, bleak mood that had been upon him while he had been at the keyhole gave way to a sense of relaxation.

He sat down with his back against a clay wall. Groping with his fingers, he opened the tool box and extracted a crowbar, a hammer, a brace, a bit and a screwdriver and fixed them securely about his body, like a soldier arming himself for battle. Yes, he would tunnel his way through walls now and perhaps dig his way into some place where he could find food. It was night and perhaps the sound of his digging would not be heard. He went along the wall, tapping the butt of the screwdriver softly against the brick. He paused, reasoning: There should be other basements farther on. He got his crowbar from his belt and tried to loosen a bit of cement. He had no luck and he brought out the screwdriver and used it as a chisel, striking the hammer lightly against its head. He succeeded in dislodging two bricks. Sweating, he wielded the hammer and as each brick came loose he piled it behind him. After slowly removing two layers, he found himself confronting plastering.

He braced himself, expecting the unknown, chipping away softly with the crowbar. Suddenly, a steady stream of fresh air came to him. Go easy now, he told himself. He caught a faint roar of faraway sound. What was that? Groping in blackness, he made the hole larger, poised at any moment to rise and flee to the sewer. A tiny lump of coal tumbled toward him; he made the hole still larger and discovered that he was digging into a basement coal bin. When the hole was big enough to admit his body, he climbed through, elbowing aside the coal; he scrambled forward and found that he was directly under a pipe. The roaring noise was a trifle louder now, but he could not identify it. Grasping the pipe with both hands, he worked his body out and then swung down, hanging by his fingers, his feet dancing in black space. How deep was the drop? He was afraid to let go. The muscles of his arms were aching and he thought rapidly. Should he let himself drop? The distance may be ten, twenty, or a hundred feet. . . . Hand over hand, he walked outward on the pipe and he heard the sound of many voices. *Where was he?* The voices did not sound like those he had heard in the church; it was more like a baseball game. He had an idea. Hanging by his left hand, he searched quickly through his pockets with his right hand to find some trifle to drop below to tell him how far it was to the ground. He found a dime—he could tell by the fine ridges around its edge—and let it drop. It tinkled quickly and faintly. Can't be far, he reasoned. He loosened his fingers and hit abruptly upon a concrete floor, his nostrils full of fresh air, his ears assaulted by the sound of many voices.

He ranged about on tiptoe, investigating; the rising roar of voices seemed to come from above him. Perhaps he was in the basement of a prizefight stadium? As he listened the shouting voices died to a low, constant din that did not rise or sink. Those voices lured him, as had the voices that sang hymns in the church. Yes, he had to see the faces of those people. He crept forward cautiously, his hands outstretched as usual, and his fingers touched a smooth wall and at the instant of his touching it, the waves of voices rose again and it was as though an electric button had turned the voices on when his fingers touched the wall. Oh. . . . Maybe he was listening to a radio? No; no radio he had ever heard sounded that real.

As the voices died again to a low pitch, he felt along the wall and reached a corner and followed along the length of another wall, smooth and cold. His flesh felt a pricking sensation. Where was he going? He reached another corner and paused; it seemed as though he were playing a game with some unseen person whose intelligence outstripped his, who knew what he was going to encounter before he encountered it, who knew how he was going to react before he reacted. He pushed on and his fingers, poised sensitively before him, touched a rough metal ridge in the surface of the wall. He discovered that he was feeling over the facade of a door and he touched a metal knob whose cold surface was pleasant to his sweaty palm. He put his ear to the flat plane of the door and listened; the sound of the distant voices came clearer, but he did not know if they were voices of joy or despair. His hand gripped the knob and twisted it until he heard a soft click and felt the springy weight of the door as it opened a fraction of an inch. He was afraid to open it wide, yet he was lured on by curiosity and wonder. He jerked open the door and saw a furnace glowing with red coals. Ten feet from where he stood was another door, half ajar. He went to it, passing a sink plainly visible in the red darkness. He edged himself into the doorway and peered down an empty, white, high-ceilinged corridor that terminated in a dark complex of shadow. The belling voices rolled over him and his eagerness mounted.

Unconsciously, he turned back into the red room and stared about; his impulses had become tangled and he was at a loss. His eyes fell upon the faucet and again purpose informed his actions; he went to the sink and turned the faucet and the water flowed smoothly in a silent stream that looked like a spout of blood. He brushed the mad image from his mind; then, instead of drinking, he began to wash his hands leisurely and thoroughly, becoming engrossed in the task to the extent that he looked about for the usual bar of soap. He found one and rubbed it vigorously in his palms and a rich red lather blossomed in his cupped fingers, like a scarlet sponge. He stared at the red foam like a child inspecting some new manifestation of light or movement that had come within line of its vision, then he scrubbed and rinsed his hands meticulously. He examined his wet palms and found that the tiny blister which had risen on his finger from mowing Mrs. Wooten's lawn was almost healed. He looked about for a towel, but there was none. He shut off the water and pulled off his shirt and wiped his hands dry; his fingers felt clean and supple. He put on the damp shirt and was grateful for the cool wetness that came to his skin. He wanted to see his face, but he could not find a mirror. He ran his fingers over the matted growth of hair on his chin; he needed a shave badly.

When he had turned from the door to the sink, he had slipped back—from fatigue and sleepiness—into the characteristics of everyday life aboveground; and, having been engaged in the simple act of washing his hands, he had merely taken the next step in the long ritual of routine. He fought free of the spell of habit and looked wonderingly at the sink, trying to remember what it was he had wanted to do so urgently just a few minutes before. Yes, he had wanted a drink of water. He turned on the faucet again, bowled his fingers beneath the flowing stream and, when the water bubbled over the brim of his grouped palms, he bent and pursed his lips and drank in long, slow swallows; he paused, breathing through open lips and teeth, absorbed in the sensations of his body. Finally, he shut off the water and sighed.

His bladder was tight and he faced the wall and lowered his head and fumbled with the fly of his trousers and bent his head and watched a red stream strike the concrete floor. He wrinkled his nostrils against acrid wisps of vapor; though he had been tramping in the sewer, he was particularly careful to step back and not let his wet shoes come in contact with his urine. The water he had drunk made him profoundly drowsy and he wanted to crawl off into some corner and curl up and sleep. He turned from the wall, yawned, listening to the deluge of voices. The old hunger and curiosity returned and he tiptoed slowly into the corridor and went past a shut door, wondering what he would do if someone suddenly stepped out of it. He crept on and the voices swelled louder; he reached the end of the corridor and the voices were a tumult. He came to a narrow, white stone stairway leading circularly upwards into darkness and it was from down this stairway that the tide of voices spilt in a steady volume. There was no question in his mind but that he was going to ascend those steps and see what was happening. He was so excited that the fear of encountering someone did not deter him; he had to go.

Mounting the spiraled staircase, he heard the voices roll as in a steady wave, then leap to a crescendo, only to die away, but always remaining audible. Ahead of him glowed red letters: E – X – I – T. At the top of the steps he paused in front of a black curtain that fluttered uncertainly. In slow motion his left hand parted the folds of the curtain and he eased forward and looked up into a huge, inverted bowl in whose convex depths there gleamed shimmering clusters of distant lights. Hovering in midair, level with his eyes, were many poles of bright light stabbing the hazy air. Sprawling distantly below him was a stretch of human faces, all tilted slightly upward, chanting, shouting, whistling, screaming, laughing. Dangling before these faces, high upon a screen of silver, were jerking shadows. This is a movie, he said. Slow laughter broke from his lips.

He stood in a box in the reserved section of a movie house and the impulse he had had to tell the people in the church to stop their singing seized him again. These people were *laughing* at their *lives*, at the animated shadows of themselves. Why did they not rise up and go out into the sunlight and do some deed that would make them live? Compassion translated itself into actuality; in his imagination he stepped out of the box, walked out upon the thin air, walked on down to the audience; and, hovering in air just above their heads, he stretched out his hands and tried to touch them.

His tension lessened, and he found himself back in the box, looking down into the sea of faces. No; it could not be done. He could not awaken them. He sighed; yes, they were children, sleeping in their living, awake in their dying. . . .

III

He turned away, parted the black curtain and looked out; he saw no one and walked to the white stone steps that led to the basement. When he reached the bottom of the stairs he saw a white man in trim blue uniform coming toward him. So used had his judgment become to living underground that he thought foolishly that he could walk right on past the man, as though he were a kind of ghost. Then the sheer reality of it came to him; he was real and so was this man whose grey eyes, as they came near him, were looking intently at him. He stopped and the man stopped.

"You're looking for the men's room, sir?" the man asked politely, giving a little salute; and, without waiting for a reply, he turned and pointed: "Right down this way, sir. The door to your left."

He watched the man walk up the steps and go out of sight.

He laughed silently, then went back to the basement and stood in the red shadows listening to the incessant roll of voices. He started at hearing footsteps; he crawled quickly into the coal bin. Lumps rattled noisily. The footsteps came into the basement and stopped. He waited, sweating, crouching with aching back. For a long time there was silence. Then he heard the tinny clang of metal and the room was lit to a brighter glow of red. Somebody's tending the furnace, he thought. Footsteps came closer and he grew taut. Looming before him was a white face lined with coal dust, the face of an old man with white hair and blue eyes. Highlights spotted his gaunt cheekbones and he held a huge shovel in his hands. There was a screechy scrape of metal against stone as the shovel scooted along the concrete floor. Grunting, the old man lifted a full shovel of coal and went from sight.

The red glow of the basement dimmed momentarily as coal was tossed into the fire; then a bright, yellow sheen came as the coal flared. The old man came back for more coal, but not once did he lift his eyes. As he watched the man, sweat formed into rivulets and ran down his chin, congealing into drops and splashing onto his fingers; his body was weeping tears of terror. Six times the old man came to the bin and then went to the furnace with shovels of coal. Finally the furnace door banged shut. The old man shuffled back to the coal bin with averted eyes and took out a dirty handkerchief and mopped his face. "Whew," he breathed. With palsied hand he hung the shovel upon a hook on the wall and turned and trudged slowly out of the basement. His footsteps died away.

He came to himself and stood; lumps of coal clattered down the pile. He stepped out of the bin and was surprised to see an electric bulb suspended above his head. Why had not the old man turned the light on? Oh! He understood: The old man had shoveled coal into this furnace for so many years that he had no need for light; he had lived within the narrow grooves of habit so long that he had learned to see in his dark world without the aid of eyes, like those sightless worms that inch along underground by a sense of touch.

He switched on the light and his eyes fell upon a lunch pail. He was afraid to hope that it was full. He picked it up; it was heavy. He opened it. *Sandwiches!* He glanced around; he was alone. The old man can buy some more, he mumbled. He searched farther and found a paper of matches and a half-empty tin of tobacco. He put the matches and tobacco eagerly into his pocket, clicked off the light; holding the lunch pail under his arm, he went through the door, groped the pile of coal and stood again in the basement of the undertaking establishment. Feeling and seeing with his fingers, he opened the lunch pail and ripped off a piece of paper bag and brought out the tin and spilled grains of tobacco—a lot of it tumbled over his fingers and was lost—evenly and slowly into the makeshift concave of paper. He put the tin away and carefully folded the paper around the tobacco and wet it with spittle. His mouth watered in anticipation. He inserted the clumsy cigarette into his mouth and lit it and sucked acrid smoke that bit his lungs and made his eyes water. He felt the effect of the nicotine as it reached upward to his brain and outward along his arms to his fingertips and down to his stomach and loins and along all the tired nerves of his body.

With lumpish cigarette slanting in flexed lips, he groped and re-entered the hole he had dug and lowered himself once more to the floor of the basement of the theatre. A cunning idea was in his mind. Why could he not crouch behind the coal pile and tunnel another hole into another basement? *Good!* He fumbled forward and felt a wall and poked at it with the screwdriver and the cement crumbled a bit and at once his eagerness was whetted. If he loosened enough of these bricks, what would he see? Where could he go? What would he find?

He leaned the rod beside a wall and balanced the handle of the lunch pail upon it and took out the crowbar and began to jab at the cement that sheered away easily each time he hacked, and quicker than he thought it would happen, a brick was completely loose. He pulled it out and laid it carefully at his feet and turned feverishly to the job of loosening other bricks, only to find that they were not so easy. He sighed, weak from effort. Yes, he would go back to his cave and eat and sleep and then return. He groped back to the cave and stumbled along a wall until his foot struck the tool box. He sat upon it and opened the lunch pail and took out two thick sandwiches. He smelt them. Pork chops! he exclaimed. He leaned his back against the dirt wall and closed his eyes and stretched out his legs and devoured a sandwich. All thought of loosening the bricks went from him as he savored the juicy meat and the smooth rye bread. He chewed rapidly and gulped down lumpy mouthfuls that made him long for a drink of water. When he finished the second sandwich, he found an apple and gobbled it up, sucking the core until the last taste of flavor was drained from it. He took the bones left from the chops, and, like a dog, ground them thoroughly in his teeth, enjoying the salty, tangy marrow. He finished, sighed profoundly, and surrendered his body to the digestive processes. He grew sleepy. He crawled to one side and stretched out full length on the dry ground and took the tool box for a pillow and put it under his head. It felt awkward, but he was so sleepy that the sensation of discomfort quickly left. A rush of air that was like a groan escaped his lips. . . .

. . . his body was washed by cold water that gradually turned warm and he was buoyed upon a dark stream that swept him to a sea of wild waves and suddenly he found himself walking upon the water how strange and light it was to walk over swirling currents and he came upon a nude woman holding a nude baby in her arms and the woman was sinking into the water and holding her baby high above her head and screaming *help* and he ran over the water to the woman and reached her just before she went down and he took the baby and stood watching the breaking bubbles where the woman went down and he called *lady* and there was no answer and he called again *lady* and still no answer yes dive down there and rescue that woman but he could not take this baby into the depths with him and tenderly he laid the baby on top of the water expecting it to sink but the baby floated and he leaped into the water and held his breath and strained his eyes to see through the gloomy volume of water and he opened his mouth and called *lady* and the water bubbled and his chest ached but he could not see the woman and he called again *lady lady* and again there was no answer and his feet touched sand and his chest felt about to burst and he bent his knees and propelled himself violently upwards and water rushed past his body as he shot up up up and his head bobbed out and he breathed deeply and looked around where was the baby the baby was gone and he rushed over the water looking for the baby calling *where is it* but as far as he could see the water was empty and the sea and the sky and the water threw back an echo *where is it* and he began to doubt that he could stand upon the water and then he was sinking and as he struggled the water grew turbulent and rushed him downward spinning dizzily and he opened his mouth to call for help and water rushed into his lungs and he choked. . . .

IV

He groaned and leaped erect in the dark, his eyes wide. The images of terror that thronged his brain would not let him sleep. He rose, sure that the tools were still hitched to his belt, and groped his way to the coal pile and found the rectangular gap from which he had taken the brick. He took out the crowbar and hacked. Then dread paralyzed him. How long had he slept? Was it day or night now? He had to be careful; someone might hear him if it were day. He scraped for hours at the cement, working silently. Faintly quivering above him was the dim sound of the yelling voices. He cocked his head. Crazy people, he muttered, smiling. Having rested, the digging was not difficult now. He soon had a dozen bricks out. His spirits rose.

He took out another brick and his fingers probed empty space. *Good!* But what lay ahead of him? Another basement? He made the hole larger and climbed through; he walked

over an uneven floor and felt a metal surface. He listened for
sounds; there were none. He struck a match and saw that he
was standing behind a furnace in a basement; before him,
on the far side of the room, was a door. He opened it; it was
full of odds and ends. Light spilled through a window above
his head. Then he was aware of a soft, continuous tapping.
What was it? He placed a chair beneath the window, stood
upon it, and looked out into an areaway. He eased the window up and crawled through. He looked upward at a series
of window ledges. He glanced about to assure himself that he
was alone. The sound of the tapping came sharply now. Somebody's using a typewriter. . . . It was coming from above him.
He grasped the prongs of a rain pipe and hoisted himself; the
tapping was distinct. Oh! Through a half-inch opening of window he saw a doorknob about three feet from him. No, it was
not a doorknob; it was a tiny, circular disc of stainless steel
with many fine markings upon it. He held his breath; he saw
an eerie white hand, seemingly detached from its arm, touch
the metal knob and twirl it, first to left, then to right. It was
the dial of a safe! Suddenly he could see the dial no more; a
huge metal door swung slowly toward him and he was looking
into a safe full of green wads of paper money, rows of coins
wrapped in brown paper, and jars and boxes of various sizes.
His heart quickened. Good Lord. . . . The white hand went in
and out of the safe, taking wads of bills and cylinders of coins.
The hand vanished and he heard a muffled click as the metal
door closed. Only the steel dial was visible now. The continuous sound of the typewriter still tapped in his ears. He blinked
his eyes, wondering if this was real, and waited for the white

hand to show again. His heart beat slowly and heavily; he bit his lips.

Still clinging to the rain pipe, he looked about the areaway; he saw no one. A daring idea came to him and he pulled the screwdriver from his belt. If the white hand twirled that dial again, he could see how far to the right and left the dial spun and he would have the combination! His blood tingled. I can scratch the numbers here. . . . Holding the pipe with one hand, he made the sharp edge of the screwdriver bite into the brick wall with the other. Yes, he could do it. He waited for a long time, but the white hand did not return. Goddamn! Had he been more alert, he could have counted the twirls and he would have had the combination! He got down and stood in the areaway, wrapped in reflection.

How could he get into that room? He climbed through the window and stood again in the basement and saw wooden stairs leading upward. Maybe that was the room in which someone was typing? The room where the safe stood? Thinking that the white hand was now fingering the steel dial, he pulled himself again through the window and climbed the rain pipe and peered through; he saw only the dial glinting in the yellow glow of an unseen electric light.

He got down, doubled his fists. Well, he would explore that basement. He went back and mounted the wooden steps to a door; he peered through a keyhole; all was dark, though the tapping was around or above him. He turned the knob and the door swung in; he looked into a room filled with crates; along a wall was a table upon which were many radios lying in disorder amid electrical tools. Looks like a radio shop, he muttered.

Well, he could rig up a radio in the cave. He found a sack, slid a radio into it, and slung it across his back. Closing the door, he went down the steps and stood again in the basement, disappointed. He had not solved the problem of the dial and he was irked. He set the radio on the floor and again hoisted himself through the window and up the rain pipe and squinted; the metal door was swinging shut. Goddamn! How could he get into that room? He could jimmy the window, but it would be better if he could get in without leaving any trace. He lowered himself into the basement. To the right of him, he calculated, should be the building that held the safe; therefore, if he dug a hole *here*, he ought to reach his goal. He began a quiet scraping; it was hard work, for the bricks were not damp. He eventually got one out and lowered it to the floor. He had to be careful; perhaps people were beyond the wall. For two hours he worked in the darkness, loosening bricks until he had made a fairly large hole. How thick was this wall? Seeing with his fingers, he extracted a second layer of brick, but there was still another. He was ready to surrender. I'll dig one more, he resolved. When the next brick came out, he felt air. He waited to be challenged, but nothing happened.

He enlarged the hole and pulled himself through and stood in quiet darkness. He scratched a match to flame and saw steps; he mounted them and peered through a keyhole: daylight. He strained to hear the typewriter. Maybe the office was closed? He twisted the knob and the door swung in and a frigid blast made him shiver. In the dimness were halves and quarters of pigs and steers hanging from metal hooks on a ceiling, red meat encased in layers of white fat. Fronting him was frost-coated glass from behind which came indistinguishable sounds. The floor was covered with sawdust that held clotted pools of blood. The odor of fresh raw meat sickened him and he backed away, his hand still on the knob. A meat market, he whispered.

Light flooded the room and he tensed himself. The red-white meat was drenched in a yellow glare. The door opened and a white man wearing a crimson-spotted jacket came in and took down a bloody meat cleaver. He eased the door to, holding it ajar just enough to watch the man. He hoped the darkness in which he stood would keep him from being seen. The man took a hunk of steer and placed it upon a bloody wooden block and bent forward and whacked it with the cleaver. The man's face was hard, square, grim; a tiny jet of mustache smudged his upper lip and a cowlick of black hair fell over his left eye. Each time he lifted the cleaver and brought it down he let out a short, deep-chested grunt. After he had cut the meat, he wiped blood off the block with a sticky wad of gunny sack and hung the cleaver upon a hook. His face was proud as he placed the meat in the crook of his elbow and left.

The door slammed; once more he was in the dark. His tension subsided. From behind the frost-coated glass he heard the man's voice: "Twenty-eight cents a pound, ma'am . . ." He shuddered, feeling that there was something he had to do. But what? He stepped forward and looked at the steel cleaver. He sneezed and was terrified lest the man hear him and return.

He took down the cleaver and squinted at the sharp edge of the steel blade smeared with cold blood. Behind the ice-coated glass a cash register rang with a vibrant, musical tinkle. He rubbed the glass with his thumb and cleared a spot that enabled him to see into the front of the store. The shop was empty, save for the man who was now putting on his hat and coat. He grasped the meat cleaver and walked briskly through the door into the basement and groped his way to the hole behind the furnace and stood with his hand about the handle of the cleaver, breathing softly. He struck a match and held it near the sharp, steel blade; red blobs of blood fascinated and repelled him. His fingers tightened about the handle with all the force of his body; he wanted to fling it from him, but he knew he could not. The match flame wavered and fled; he climbed through the hole and put the cleaver in the sack with the radio. Yes, he would keep it, for what purpose he did not know.

He was about to leave, then remembered the safe. *Where was it?* Opposite the last hole he had dug, he plied the crow-bar, made another hole, and pulled himself through. His nostrils filled with the fresh scent of coal. He struck a match; yes, he was in a basement and the usual steps led upward. He tip-toed to a door and eased it open. A blue-eyed white girl stood in front of a steel cabinet, her blue eyes falling on him. She turned chalk white and she gave a high-pitched scream and swayed. He bounded down the steps and raced to his hole and clambered through, replacing the bricks with nervous haste. He paused, hearing loud voices.

"What's the matter, Alice?"

"A *man* . . ."

"What man?"

"A man was in the door . . ."

"Oh, nonsense!"

"He was looking through the door!"

"Aw, you're dreaming . . ."

"I *did* see a man!"

The girl was crying now.

"There's nobody here."

Another man's voice sounded.

"What is it, Bob?"

"Alice says a man was here."

"Come on. Let's take a look."

He waited, poised for flight. Footsteps descended the stairs.

"There's nobody down here."

"The window's locked."

"And there's no door . . ."

"She's seeing things."

"You ought to fire her. She's hysterical. She ought to get married."

The men laughed. Footsteps sounded again on the steps. A door slammed. He sighed. But his glimpse of the room had been too brief. Was the safe in there? He had to know. Boldly he groped through once more. He reached the steps and pulled off his shoes and tiptoed up and peered through the keyhole. His head accidentally touched the door; it swung silently in a fraction of an inch, and he saw the girl bent over the cabinet, her back to him. Beyond her was the safe. He turned, tiptoed back down the steps. I found it, he thought exultantly.

Now he had to get the combination. Even if the window was locked, he could gain access to the room when the office closed. He slithered through the holes he had dug and stood again in the basement where he had left the radio; again he crawled out of the window and lifted himself up the rain pipe and peered. The steel dial shone. Resigned to a long wait, he returned to the basement and sat with his back against a wall. From faraway came faint sounds of the life aboveground; once he looked with a puzzled expression at the dark sky above his head. Frequently he rose and climbed the pipe to see the white hand open the dial, but nothing happened. He trembled with impatience. It was not the money that was luring him, but the fact that he could get it with impunity, without risking reprisal. Was the hand now twirling the dial . . . ? He rose and mounted the rain pipe and looked, but the hand was not in sight. He sat again with a heavy sigh.

Perhaps it would be better if he clung to the pipe and watched continuously. He lifted himself and squinted at the dial until his eyes thickened with tears. Exhausted, he stood again in the areaway. He heard a door being shut and he clawed up the pipe and looked. He jerked tense as a vague figure passed in front of him. He stared unblinkingly, hugging the pipe with one hand and holding the screwdriver ready to write upon the brick wall with the other. His ears caught: *dong . . . dong . . . dong . . . dong . . . dong . . .* five o'clock, he muttered. Maybe they were closing now. Perhaps the safe was *already* locked! He bit his lip in exasperation; then, just as he was about to give up, the hand touched the steel dial and twirled it once to right and stopped. He squinted and etched l-R-6 upon the wall with the tip of the screwdriver. The hand twirled the dial twice toward left and stopped at two and he engraved 2-L-2 upon the wall. The dial was spun four times to right and stopped at six again; he wrote 4-R-6. The dial rotated three times to left and was centered straight up and down and he wrote 3-L-0. The hand went from view and the door swung open; again he saw piles of green money and rows of wrapped coins. I got it, he said.

Then he was astonished. There were now two hands. The right hand lifted a wad of green bills and deftly slipped it up the sleeve of the left hand. The white hands trembled. Again the right hand went into the safe and picked up a wad of bills and pushed it quickly up the sleeve of the left hand. He's stealing, he said. He grew indignant, as if he owned the money. Though *he* had planned to steal the money, he despised and pitied the man. His stealing the money and the man's stealing the money were entirely two different things. He wanted to steal the money merely for the sensation involved, and he had no intention of ever spending a penny of it; but the man who was now stealing it was going to spend it, perhaps for pleasure. The hands went away and the huge steel door closed with a soft click.

Though angry, he was satisfied. They would close the office soon. I'll clean the place out, he mused. He imagined the entire office staff upset; the police would question everyone for a crime they had not committed, just as they had once questioned him. And they would have no idea of how the money had been taken until they discovered the holes he had tunneled in the wall of the basements. He lowered himself and laughed mischievously, with the glee of an adolescent boy.

He kept vigil at the window until the yellow light went out. They're closed now, he said. He flattened himself against the brick wall as the window above him shut with a rasping noise; he heard a series of metallic clicks. He looked; the window had been bolted with a metal shutter. That won't help you, he whispered, smiling. He went back into the basement and picked up the sack containing the radio and cleaver, and crawled through the two holes he had dug and groped his way into the basement; he saw and heard nothing. He moved in slow motion, breathing softly. Careful, he thought.

In his memory was the combination written in bold white characters as upon a blackboard. Eel-like, he squeezed through and landed on the concrete floor. Careful. . . . He tiptoed up, tried the knob and pushed the door in slowly. Then his courage ebbed; his imagination wove dangers.

Perhaps someone was waiting in there, ready to shoot? He dangled his cap on a forefinger and pushed it past the jamb of the door. If anyone fired, they would shoot his cap first. He widened the door, holding the crowbar above his head, ready to beat off an assailant. The rumble of a streetcar brought him to himself; he entered the room. Moonlight streaked in through a side window. He confronted the safe, then checked himself. Better look around. . . . He stepped to a closed door. Perhaps someone was hiding in there? He opened it and saw a small washbowl and a faucet. He opened another door and saw a dark, seemingly empty room. He closed the door again and turned back to the safe and fingered the dial and found that it moved with ease. Then he laughed and spun the dial just for the fun of it.

He set to work. . . . He turned the dial to the figures he saw upon the blackboard of his memory. It was ridiculously easy, so easy that he thought that maybe the safe had not been locked. The heavy door eased loose. He caught hold of the handle and pulled hard, but the door swung with a momentum of its own. Breathless, he gaped inside at the piles of green bills, the long rows of wrapped coins. He glanced guiltily over his shoulder; it seemed impossible that someone should not call him to stop, brand him guilty. . . .

What place is this? He wondered. He noticed for the first time the black lettering that curved in reverse across the window. He spelled out: HILLMAN AND SWANSON. REAL ESTATE AND INSURANCE. They'll be some surprised when they open up in the morning, he thought. Yes; he remembered the firm; it collected hundreds of thousands of dollars in rent from poor colored folks; now he was taking just a little of it, not to spend, but just to keep around and look at. He held open the top of the sack and lifted up a thick, heavy, compactly tied wad of green money; the bills were crisp and new and he admired the clean-cut edges. Washington sure knows how to make this stuff, he mumbled. He rubbed the money with his fingers, as though expecting it suddenly to reveal secret qualities. It's just like any other kind of paper, he observed with a musing smile. He lifted the wad to his nose and smelt the fresh odor of ink, then he dropped the wad into the sack and picked up another.

As he toyed with the money, there was in him no sense of possessiveness; he was intrigued with the shape and form and color of it, with the manifold reactions and attitudes he knew that men and women held toward it. He had put several wads into the sack when it occurred to him to examine the denominations of the bills; he had already, without noticing it, put in many wads of one-dollar bills. Aw, shucks, he said in disgust. There were many wads of one-hundred-dollar bills. Yeah, take the big ones, he said, laughing. He dumped the one-dollar bills upon the floor and grabbed all the hundred-dollar wads he could find and swept them into the sack; then he raked in the rolls of coins with crooked fingers. He looked around; he had not heard a single noise since he had been in the office. He backed away and pushed the safe door and it swung shut with its heavy, slow weight.

He walked to a desk upon which sat a typewriter. He was fascinated with the machine; never in his life had he used one of them. It was a queer instrument, something beyond the rim of his life. Whenever he had been in an office where a girl was typing, he had always involuntarily spoken in whispers. As he had seen others do, he inserted a sheet of paper into the machine. It went in lopsided but he did not know how to straighten it. Spelling in a soft, diffident voice, he pecked his name on the keys: *freddaniels*. He looked at it and laughed.

Yes, he would take the typewriter too. He lifted the machine and placed it atop of the bulk of money. He did not feel that he was stealing, for the cleaver, the radio, and the money were on the same level of value, all meant the same thing to him. They were the toys of the men who lived in the dead world of sunshine and rain he had left, the world that had condemned him. He contemplated his loot for a long time, then went to the washroom, got a towel and tied the sack tightly. Then he looked up and was momentarily frightened by his shadow looming on the wall in front of him.

He lifted the sack, descended the steps and lugged it across the basement, gasping for breath. Finally he stood in the cave, brooding about the items he had stolen, and he remembered the singing in the church, the people yelling in the theatre, the dead baby, and the nude man stretched out cold upon the white table. . . . He saw these things hovering before his eyes and he felt that some dim meaning tied them together, that some magical relationship made them kin. He stared with vacant eyes, convinced that all of these images, with their tongueless reality, were striving to tell him something.

V

Seeing with his fingers, he emptied the sack and set each item neatly upon the earth floor. Exploring farther, he took the bulb, the socket, and the wire out of the tool chest; he was elated to find a double socket on one end of the wire. He crammed the stuff into his pocket and hoisted himself upon the rusty pipes and looked through the slit; the church was dim and empty. Somewhere in this wall were live electric wires. But where? He lowered himself, groped and tapped the brick wall lightly with the butt of the screwdriver, listening vainly for hollow sounds. I'll just take a chance, he said.

He tried for an hour to dislodge a brick, but with no success. He struck a match and found that he had dug a depth of only an inch! No use in fooling with this, he said with a sigh. He looked upward in the flickering light of the match, then lowered his eyes, only to glance up again, startled. Directly above his head was a wealth of electric wiring running along the entire length of the low ceiling. I'll be damned, he said, snickering.

He got an old, dull knife from the tool box and, seeing with his fingers, separated the two strands of wire and cut away the insulation. Twice he received a slight shock. He scraped the wiring clean and managed to join the twin-ends of the wires, then screwed in the bulb. The sudden illumination blinded him and he shut his lids to kill the pain in his eyeballs. I got that done, he thought jubilantly.

With the bulb and socket in hand, he walked back to the dirt cave and placed the bulb on the floor. The light cast a blatant glare on the bleak clay walls. Next he plugged one end of the wire that dangled from the radio into the light socket and bent down and switched on the button; almost at once there was the harsh sound of static, but no words or music. How come it don't work? he asked himself.

He toyed with the dials of the radio and wondered if he had damaged the mechanism in any way. Perhaps it needed grounding? He rummaged in the chest, found another length of wire, fastened it to the ground of the radio, then tied the opposite end to a rusty pipe. Rising and growing distinct, a slow strain of music entranced him with its measured sound. He placed the tool chest against the wall and sat, deliriously happy.

He searched again in the tool chest and found a half-gallon can of glue; he opened it and smelt a sharp odor. Then he remembered that he had not even looked at the money. He took a wad of green bills out of the sack and weighed it in his palm. He broke the seal and held one of the bills up to the light and studied it closely. *The United States of America will pay to the bearer on demand one hundred dollars*, he read in slow speech; and then: *This note is legal tender for all debts public and private....* He broke into a slow, musing laugh. He felt that he was reading of the petty doings of people who lived on some far-off planet. He turned the bill over and saw a beautiful white building with soaring columns and wide, curving steps leading up to an imposing entrance. He had no desire to count the money; it was what it stood for—all the manifold currents of life swirling aboveground—that captivated him. Next he opened up the rolls of coins and let them slide from their paper wrappings to the ground; the gleaming pennies and nickels and dimes piled high in front of him, a bright mound of shimmering silver and copper. He sifted a few of the coins through his fingers, listening to their tinkle as they struck the conical pile.

He got the typewriter and pulled it forward and took a sheet of paper and inserted it and typed: *itwasalonghotday....* He looked at it and was determined to type the sentence without making any mistakes. But how did one make capital letters? He experimented and luckily found how to lock the machine for capital letters and then shift back to lowercase. Next he learned how to make spaces. Then he wrote correctly and carefully: *It was a long hot day*. The sheet was dirty and he took it out and inserted another and retyped the sentence in neat, black characters without making a single error. Just why he picked that particular sentence, he did not know; it was merely the ritual of performing the thing. Holding in his hand the white sheet with the single sentence printed across its middle, he looked around, neck stiff, eyes hard, and spoke to some imaginary person:

"Yes, I'll have the contracts ready tomorrow."

He laughed. That's just the way they talk, he said to himself. He grew weary of the game and pushed the machine aside. His eyes fell upon the can of glue and a mischievous idea bloomed in him, filling him with nervous eagerness. He leaped up and opened the can of glue, then untied the sack and broke open the wads of bills. I'm going to have some wallpaper, he said with a luxurious, physical laugh that made him bend at the knees. He took the towel with which he tied the sack and balled it into a swab and dipped it into the can and dabbed glue onto the wall; then he pasted one green bill neatly by the side of another. He stepped back and cocked his head. Jesus! That's funny . . . ! He slapped his thighs and guffawed. He had triumphed over the world aboveground. He was *free*! He re-membered how he had hugged the few dollars Mrs. Wooten had given him and he wanted to run from the underground and yell his discovery to the world.

He finally controlled his laughter and swabbed all the dirt walls of the cave with glue and pasted them with green bills; when he finished, he stood in the center of the room and mar-veled—the walls blazed with an indescribable yellow-green fire. Yes, this room would be his main hideout; between him and the world that had rejected him would stand this mocking symbol. He had not stolen the money; he had simply taken it, just as a man would pick up firewood in a forest. And that was how the world aboveground now seemed to him, a wild forest filled with death, stalked by blind animals.

The walls of money finally palled on him and he grew sleepy, but there was no fun in using a tool box for a pillow. As he sat there nodding he found himself wanting to start out exploring in the sewers, and wanting to lie down and take a nap. The impulse to wander prevailed and he rose and clicked off the light and radio and went to the opening and climbed through and stood in the glassy water, watching the checkered pattern wrought by the light falling from the manhole cover. He sloshed with the rod for a quarter of an hour and suddenly, when he put his right foot forward at a street intersection, he fell backward and shot down violently into the grey water. In a spasm of terror his right hand clutched the rod and he felt the streaking water tugging at his body. The current reached his neck and for a moment he was stationary; his chest heaved and it was some time before he realized what had happened to him. He had dropped into a down-curve and had saved himself only because the rod had caught on either side of the hole. He took quick stock of his plight; if he moved clumsily he might be sucked under after all. He grasped the rod with both hands and slowly worked himself over to one side of the down-curve and grabbed hold of a concrete edge. He heaved a deep sigh and pulled himself up and stood again in the sweeping water; he peered about, thankful that he had missed death.

He picked up the rod again and resolved to be more careful. He pushed ahead, going slower this time. The tunnel grew wider and higher and was pitch black. He went forward cautiously and his head bumped into a low-hanging obstruction. He felt upwards and encountered an iron pipe and he followed it to a wall and felt that the bricks that surrounded it were loose. He reasoned that this pipe ran back into the dirt and entered some basement. Suppose he tunneled forward around it? He took out his crowbar, pried the bricks out, and hewed at the dirt, racking out lumps with his bare hands; it was slow work and sweat dripped from his chin. He longed for a shovel, for that would have made the digging easier. Should he go back into one of those basements and get one? No; that meant wading again in that foul and dangerous sewer. He dug on some five feet, lying flat on his stomach, pushing clods of earth behind him into the sewer. At last he came to a brick wall; his muscles were aching. Despite the fact that the bricks were damp, they were much harder than the ones he had tried before. An hour's toiling in the darkness loosened two bricks; the others came easier then and soon he made a wide hole. He heard the faint, distant sound of voices. The tone and accent were those of white men.

"Where're you going tonight, Bob?"

"I think the wife and I'll get into the old bus and drive up somewhere along the seashore."

"Yeah. My old lady and I were up there Sunday. It's beautiful."

"I'll say it is. Where're you going?"

"Aw, I don't know. I was thinking of taking in a movie."

The voices stopped; he lay a long time, listening, staring into the black rectangular hole from which the brick had come. Working again in silent slow-motion, he proceeded to take out the other brick and soon had a hole large enough for his body to crawl through. Then, accidentally, a brick slid from his grasp and dropped with a clatter to an invisible floor. He waited to hear a challenging shout, but nothing happened. He climbed out of the hole and stood up in a dark space; he struck a match and found that he was in a storage locker. He found a door, pried the lock, and entered a basement and was surprised to see at the far end of the room faint streaks of daylight. His muscles jerked taut as he heard a heavy door banging shut. From somewhere above him came the echo of footsteps. He grabbed the iron pipe and hoisted himself upward and waited to see if anyone was coming. The footsteps died away in the distance and he swung down again to the floor and looked around. Near him was a huge furnace and a coal bin. He walked forward and saw high up in a wall an open window through which fresh air and dingy light came.

He explored the basement, walking twice past a sofa without seeing it; when he discovered it he sat upon it and the old rusty springs creaked. It was good to sit down this way, to relax upon something soft; he had not sat in a chair since the police had third-degreed him. He threw his legs upon the sofa and stretched out full length and rested his head in the crook of his arm and a mountain of fatigue weighed upon his eyes and forehead. He dozed but his imagination was alert. He saw himself rising and slowly mounting the basement steps and then opening a door and looking into a room filled with policemen. He jumped awake; he was still lying stretched on the sofa; he had not moved. He closed his eyes again and this time his anxious imagination made him feel that he was standing in a room watching over his own black, nude, waxen body lying stiff upon a white table. At the far end of the room a crowd of people huddled in a corner, fearful of his body. Though lying asleep upon the table, he stood at his side, warding the people off, guarding his body and laughing to himself as he observed the situation. They scared of me, he thought proudly. It was good that they were afraid of him, for their fear gave him respite and he drifted to sleep.

He awakened with a start, leaped to his feet, and stood at the center of the concrete floor staring, gasping. It was a full minute before he moved. He hovered between sleeping and waking, unprotected, a prey of wild fears. One part of him was asleep; his blood coursed slowly and his flesh was numb. On the other hand he was roused to a high pitch of tension; he lifted his fingers to his face and hysteria seethed in him.

Gradually he lowered his hands and struck a match. Yeah, he mumbled. How long had he slept? The question occurred to him in a vague kind of way. He did not see the green-papered walls; it was as though he was deaf and blind. He expected to see a door through which he could walk, but there was no door. He shook his head and remembered where he was. The match flame died and it was dark again. He struck still another match and saw steps leading upward; a strong gust of wind blew out the flame. He rose and mounted the steps and felt for the usual door, but could not reach it; he lifted his right foot to walk on up the steps and his shoe came down on a wooden floor with a resounding bang. He was terrified. Then he realized what had happened: The door was open and he had walked up the steps and through it and into a room and had stomped his foot on the floor, thinking that he was still mounting steps. Where was he? Should he strike another match? He felt in his pockets; he had only one left.

He groped about and encountered smooth, complex objects that felt like steel machines of some kind. Baffled, he touched a wall and tried to find an electric switch. He had to strike a match. He knelt and struck it, cupping the flame near the floor. The place seemed a factory with many rows of benches and there were several bulbs with green shades suspended from the ceiling. He turned on a light and saw a pack of cigarettes lying on a bench, which he appropriated. There were stools at the benches and he concluded that men worked here at some trade. He walked about and picked up many packets of matches and also stuffed them into his pockets. If only he could find more cigarettes! He could not make out what kind of shop this was. On the benches were many small motors; the place resembled a shoe shop in some respects, only there were no shoes in evidence and the machines were much smaller than those he had seen in shoe shops.

He was about to turn out the light in preparation for leaving when he paused to examine the glinting objects in a large, uncovered glass jar. The shining bits were mixed, it seemed, with tiny white pellets of tissue paper. Some of the glinting bits looked like pieces of glass. He poked a timid finger into the glass jar and scooped up some of the gleaming particles. Quickly, he dropped the stuff back into the jar and wiped his hands on his trousers. Maybe some kind of acid, he said with a shudder. A big metal box caught his eye and he picked it up and shook it and a dry, tinny rattle came to his ears; he brought out his screwdriver and pried the box open and lifted the lid. *Rings. . . !* His breath stopped in astonishment, then he ran about the room, noticing many things he had not noticed before. On many of the benches hung golden watches which he grabbed and rammed into his pockets. He returned to the box of rings and stared. Were these rings worth anything? He held one directly under a light and white and blue sparks of fire shot fitfully from the limpid stone as he turned it slowly in his fingers. He frowned and looked toward the front and tried to read a faint smear of lettering on a glass pane but a red neon sign flickered on and off and he could not make out all of the letters. He spelled: Jew. . . . Must be a jewelry shop, he said. He bent over the jar again and stared at the white pellets of paper and the glittering bits of glass. His lips formed an O and he breathed: Diamonds. . . . Yes, some of the diamonds were wrapped and some were bare. His heart raced with excitement.

He put the jar under his left arm and held the box in the fingers of his left hand and turned out the light and crept down the steps into the darkness of the basement. Yes, he would take this stuff to his dirt cave and examine it. Smiling, he sat the jar and box on the concrete floor and reached into his pocket and pulled out a paper of matches and struck one; there was a door to his right. Yes, he had to go inside of that door and see what was in there. He opened it; the room was dark. He advanced cautiously inside and ran his fingers along the wall for the electric switch. Then he was stark still; something had *moved* in the room! What was it? Should he get out of here, taking the rings and diamonds? He waited and the ensuing silence gave him confidence to explore farther. He wanted to strike a match, but what if someone were in the room? A match flame would make him a good target. He was tense again as he heard a faint sigh and he was now convinced that there was something alive near him, some human or some animal, something that lived and breathed. Slowly, he felt farther along the wall, hoping that he would not bump into anything. Luck was with him; he found the light switch.

He fingered it for a long time; maybe someone was standing on the other side of the room with a gun, waiting for him to reveal himself? But how could he get out of here without turning on the light? If he tried to grope his way, he would be certain to stumble into something. And he *had* to get out. He knelt upon the floor and reached his arm up to the switch and flicked the button. The moment the light came on he narrowed his eyes to see quickly. He sucked in his breath and his body gave a violent twitch and was still. In front of him, so close that it made him want to bound up and scream, was a human face.

The face was white and was so near that he could have reached out and touched it; if the man had opened his eyes at that moment, there was no telling what he might have done. Maybe he's dead, he thought with despair. No; the man was not dead, for he saw the chest rising and falling. Even though he was still afraid, he was a little more at ease now that he knew that he was not again in the presence of death. The man—long and raw-boned—was stretched out on his back upon a little cot, sleeping in his clothes, his head cushioned by a dirty pillow; his face, clouded by a dark stubble of beard, looked straight up to the ceiling. He stiffened in fear as the man sighed and mumbled and turned his eyes away from the light. I got to turn off that light, he thought quickly. Just as he was about to rise, he looked down and saw a gun and cartridge belt on the floor at the man's side. Then he was unable to move; he looked at the man's face again and the old feeling he had experienced so many times down there in the underground returned and he was rooted to the spot. This poor night watchman's job was to kill or lay down his life to protect those rings and diamonds and watches. Yes, he should get up from here right now and turn out that light, but his body remained rigid. He was filled with reflection, experiencing again that high pitch of consciousness, gazing like an invisible man hovering in space upon the life that lived aboveground in the darkness of the sun. He stood up slowly; the man did not move. He decided to take the gun and the cartridge belt with him, not to use, but just to keep, as one takes a memento from a country fair. He picked up the gun and cartridge belt and clutched them in his left hand, listening to the man breathing regularly in sleep. He was about to click off the light when his eyes fell upon a photograph perched upon a chair near the man's head; it was a picture of a smiling woman shown against a background of open fields; at the woman's side were two young children, a boy and a girl. He smiled indulgently; he was overcome with compassion as he looked at the tired old man asleep with the picture of his wife and his children at his side. He could send a bullet into that man's brain, crashing through his skull, and time would be over for him. . . .

presence of mind returned and he clicked off the light, groped his way into the basement and struck a match and found the box and jar and piled them into his left arm. He made his way to the storage locker, smiling wistfully, thinking: What a fool! A man with a gun risking his precious life each night—the only life he will ever have on this earth—to protect sparkling bits of stone that looked for all the world like glass. . . . He paused at the hole and set his burden upon the floor and fastened the gun and cartridge belt about his hips; he turned his head and looked back through the darkness toward the room in which the man slept. He had an overpowering urge to go back and wake the man and tell him. . . . He took off his shirt, thinking: No, there ain't nothing nobody can do for him. . . . He wrapped the jar and box in the shirt and formed a crude bundle which he slung into the narrow opening; he then grabbed the pipe with both hands and poked his head into the hole and rammed the bundle before him until he came, exhausted and almost indifferent, to the sewer, where he could stand up.

He set the shirt-bundle in the water and leaned wearily against a slimy wall. If the idea of abandoning his hideout underground had been broached to him at that moment, if someone had told him to go back aboveground and face whatever charges were waiting to be placed against him, he could have done so with the humbleness of a chastened child; sheer physical weariness had rendered him will-less. Feeling a desire to sleep more than any ambition to explore further the strange reaches of consciousness which had gained such a mysterious hold upon him, he sighed and picked up the box and jar and waded again in the sliding, grey water. As he walked his eyelids drooped and his feet skidded over the slippery concrete bottom of the sewer and several times he had to bring himself to a state of sharp alertness to keep from tumbling headlong into the scummy current. He passed a manhole and heard rumbling noises of traffic above him, but paid it no heed; life aboveground was now something less than reality, less than sight or sound, less even than memory....

He came fully awake only when he reached the passageway leading to the dirt cave. He pushed the bundle into the opening and shoved it forward, climbed in head first and slithered along on his stomach, his hands stretched before him. He used his fingers to propel his body forward by catching hold of the pipe above him and each time he jerked himself forward he pushed the bundle with his head. When he came to the cave he tossed the bundle and heard the rings tingling against the metal sides of the box as they struck the ground beyond. He pulled himself through and stood immobile for a moment in the darkness, then groped his way along the wall until he reached the tool box; he yawned, rubbed his eyes and lay upon the ground. He gave a long gasp and went to sleep.

VI

As he slept something irritated him. He was once on the verge of waking but his tired body told him to go back to sleep. An hour later he sat bolt upright, listening intently, his heart pounding. Hovering between sleeping and waking, he heard a ceaseless murmur, like a muffled hum. His sleepiness made him confused and he looked about in the darkness, trying to locate the sound. Yes, it was coming from beyond the wall. No doubt the church members had gathered there, just as once he had gathered with others in Reverend Davis' church to sing and pray. Then the muscles of his body jerked taut as a loud, surging hymn broke forth, sonorous and magnificent in its expression of melancholy renunciation. Involuntarily, he rose to his feet, as though rising to meet his fate. Surrounded by darkness, groggy from lack of sleep, he could not resist the tides of melody that drenched him. He felt within himself a vast and old conviction seeking to rise again. It was as though he had forgotten something and, in the act of trying to remember it, could not; but still the memory lingered. He shrank with fear from this nameless feeling that was trying to capture him, for he felt that it possessed such unlimited power that, once its prisoner, he would never be free again. Violently agitated, he took a few involuntary steps forward in the dark to escape what he felt to be a physical presence bearing down unremittingly upon him. His lips and teeth were open and his eyes stared unblinkingly. A low moan broke from him and his knees buckled and he pitched forward on his stomach, his face on the ground, his fingers clawing weakly in the loose dirt.

And then a strange and new knowledge overwhelmed him: He was *all people*. In some unutterable fashion he was *all* people and they were *he*; by the identity of their emotions they were one, and he was one with them. And this was the oneness that linked man to man, in life or death. Yet even with this knowledge, this identification with others, this obliteration of self, another knowledge swept through him too, banishing all fear and doubt and loss: He now knew too the inexpressible value and importance of himself. He must assert himself; he was propelled to do something, to devise means of action by and through which he could convince those who lived aboveground of the death-like quality of their lives.

He did not think these things; he felt them through images. While lying prone on his face in the dark on the cold dirt floor, with waves of song battering at the cliffs of his consciousness, he knew that at some time in the near future he would rise up from this underground, walk forth and say something to everybody. He did not know what he would say or how; but he had no doubt that he would soon forsake this haven and emerge again. He could not question what he felt, for *he* was *it* and *it* was *he*.

VII

How long he lay in sleep he did not know, but he slept more profoundly than men sleep from physiological fatigue. During the entire time not one portion of his body moved and his flesh was icy to the touch, his palms sweaty. The church singing had stopped and in the silence and darkness that followed he really did not exist as a personality; his emotional state had reached a high point in its tensity and had suspended. As though for purposes of renewal, he had for a time gone back into the insensible world out of which life had originally sprung, and, before he could live again, hope or plan again, a regrouping of his faculties into a new personality structure would be necessary. It was an organic pause, such as one takes in breathing. During the past turbulent hours he had endured experiences which were like sucking his lungs full of air; but now, having drained the life-fostering oxygen from the air, he was expelling the residue of poison, leaving the tiny air sacs deflated, ready to be refilled.

He groaned and a drool of spittle trickled from a corner of his mouth. With effort he rolled over on his back and belched and swallowed and sighed. Reluctantly, he propped up one knee and dragged the bottom of his left foot over the ground; he allowed his leg to remain in this position as though to ease some muscular strain. Then, while still sleeping, he pulled himself to a sitting posture. Yeah, he whispered vaguely. He lifted his right hand and rubbed it nervously over his face; he blinked his eyes several times and sneezed. He was fully awake now. He sought to recapture and understand the storm of passion that had laid him low, but his mind refused to function. Rising, he lurched unsteadily and groped for the electric bulb and twisted it and the bright light pained his eyes. He blinked and looked about the floor; yes, there was the metal box of rings, the glass jar of diamonds, the bloody meat cleaver, the radio, the tool chest, and the walls plastered with green bills glowing in the yellow light. He laughed when he saw the pile of copper and silver coins glittering beside him. He had forgotten these things and quiet amazement crept into him as he saw them again. They seemed to stand for events that had happened in another life. The old tensity which had driven him to seek so many experiences was now gone and he seemed to be in the grip of forces stemming not from his body, but from without, from this yellow light, these shimmering coins, these walls of green fire, this bloody blade of steel; and he felt that the true identity of these forces would slowly reveal themselves, not only to him but also to others. Once or twice he made an effort to take hold of himself, to shake off this weird feeling, to go back to his former state, for he was afraid of this strange land; but the task of eluding these new forces was difficult and he shrugged his shoulders in surrender.

He felt in his pocket for a cigarette and was astonished when he pulled forth a fistful of ticking golden watches that dangled by gleaming chains. Idly he stared at them, then he began to wind them up; he did not even attempt to set any of them at a certain hour, for there was no time for him now. After he had wound them carefully his eyes strayed over the green-papered walls and a slow, mocking smile formed on his lips. He was as sorry for himself as he looked at that money as he had been for the man he had seen stealing it; his memory was merged with the lives of others and he no longer appreciated the mood of high deviltry that had bubbled in him when he had decorated the walls. But, since he had the watches in his possession, he had to dispose of them in some way. He held the watches and heard their awful ticking and he hated them; these watches were measuring time, making men tense and taut with the sense of passing hours, telling tales of death, crowning time the king of consciousness.

He turned to the tool box and took out a handful of nails and a hammer and he drove the nails into the papered walls and hung the watches upon them, letting them swing down by their glittering chains, ticking busily against the background of green bills with the lemon sheen of the electric light shining upon the metal watch casings, converting discs of yellow into blobs of liquid. Hardly had he hung up the last watch when the idea upon which he had been working extended itself; he took more nails from the tool box and went around the walls and drove them through the green paper and then took the box of rings and went from nail to nail and hung up the gold bands. The white and blue diamonds sparkled with quiet and brittle laughter, as though enjoying a hilarious secret. The room had a bizarre and ghostly aspect; the yellow light tinged the green money with a fiery cast and, against this blazing backdrop, the gold of the rings and watches, and the blue-white laughter of the diamonds, leaped burningly to life.

He was suddenly conscious of the gun sagging at his hip and he drew it from the holster. He had seen men fire guns in movies, but somehow his life had never led him to contact with firearms. A desire to feel the sensation others felt in firing a gun came over him. Someone might hear. . . . But if they did, they would not know where the shot had come from. Not in their wildest imagination would they think that it came from *under the streets*! He tightened his finger on the trigger; there was a deafening report and it seemed that the entire underground had fallen upon his eardrums and in the same instant there flashed an orange-blue spurt of flame that died quickly but lingered on as a vivid afterimage. He smelt the acrid odor of burnt powder filling his lungs. Abruptly he dropped the gun.

The intensity of his emotions ebbed and he picked up the gun and hung it upon a nail on the wall; then he hung up the cartridge belt. He saw the jars of diamonds and at once he had another idea. He lifted the jars and turned them bottom upwards and the entire contents dumped upon the ground. One by one he picked them up and peeled the tissue paper from them and piled them in a neat heap. He wiped his sweaty hands dry on his trousers, lit a cigarette, and commenced playing another game. He was a rich man who lived aboveground in the black sunshine and he was strolling through a beautiful park of a summer morning, smiling, nodding to his neighbors, sucking an after-breakfast cigar. Many times he crossed the floor of the cave, avoiding the diamonds with his feet, yet subtly gauging his footsteps so that his shoes, wet with sewer slime, would strike the diamonds at some undetermined moment. After five minutes of sauntering, his right foot smashed into the neat heap and the diamonds lay scattered in all directions, glinting at him with a million tiny chuckles of icy laughter. Oh, shucks, he mumbled in mock regret, intrigued by the damage he had wrought. He continued walking, ignoring the brittle fire. He felt that he had locked deep within his heart a glorious triumph.

He flung the diamonds more evenly over the dirt floor and they showered rich sparks, collaborating with him. He went over the floor and trampled the stones just deep enough for them to be faintly visible, as though they were set delicately in the prongs of a thousand rings. A baleful, icy glare bathed the cave. He sat on the chest, lit a cigarette, frowned, and shook his head. Maybe *any*thing's right, he mumbled. Yes, if the world as men had made it was right, then anything else was right, too. Any action a man took to satisfy himself—theft or murder or torture—was right. To banish such thoughts, he turned on the radio. A melancholy piece of music rose. Brooding over the diamonds on the floor was like looking up into a sky full of stars; the illusion melted into its opposite: He was high up in the air looking down at the twinkling lights of a sprawling city. The music ended and a man recited news events. In the same attitude in which he had contemplated the city, so now, as he heard the cultivated tone, he looked down upon the land and the sea as men fought, as cities were razed, as armies marched or planes scattered bombs upon open towns, as long lines of trenches wavered and broke. He heard the names of generals and the names of towns and the names of rivers and the names and numbers of divisions that were reported in action on different fronts. He saw black smoke billowing from the stacks of warships that neared each other over wastes of water and he heard them speak the language of death as flame belched from their huge guns and red-hot shells screamed across the surface of the night seas. He saw hundreds of planes whirling and droning in the air and heard the clatter of machine-guns as they battled each other and he saw planes blazing and smoking as they fell. He saw steel tanks rumbling across fields of ripe wheat to meet other tanks and there was a loud clang of steel against steel as numberless tanks collided. He saw troops with fixed bayonets charging in waves against other troops who held fixed bayonets and men groaned as steel ripped into their bodies and they went down to die. . . . The voice of the radio died and he was looking down at the diamonds that twinkled on the floor before him.

When the spell left him he found that he was standing on his feet, staring in horror. His hovering in midair and looking down upon the reasonlessness of human life made him understand that no compassion of which the human heart was capable could ever respond adequately to that awful sight. Outside of time and space, he looked down upon the earth and saw that each fleeting day was a day of dying, that men died slowly with each passing moment as much as they did in war, that human grief and sorrow were utterly insufficient to this vast, dreary spectacle.

His failure to summon up feelings that could do justice to what he saw and felt, his sense of emptiness in the face of this stark tragedy, culminated in an all-powerful passion of guilt; his own weakness when confronted with this supreme challenge condemned and consumed him with a boundless sense of contrition. Yes, the only being who could possibly gaze down upon such a hopeless spectacle and encompass its meaninglessness would have to be a god. That was it! Maybe men had invented gods to feel what they could not feel, and they found comfort in the pity of their gods for them . . . ! For men were overwhelmed with shame and guilt when they looked down upon the irremediable frailty of their lives.

He felt that soon he would be catapulted from the underground, or he would rush headlong and crash his head in frenzied despair against the green-papered walls. He buried his face in his grimy hands.

VIII

He shut off the radio, groped his way back to the chest, and sat, fighting against an irrational compulsion to act. He rose and walked about aimlessly, touching the walls with his fingertips. The crazy walls filled him with an urge to climb out into the streets and he doused the light to escape it. He lit another cigarette and the flickering glare of his match illuminated the glittering room. Quickly he blew out the flame and climbed through by the pipe and stood again in the dashing, grey water of the sewer with the rod in his hands and the cigarette jutting from his lips. He walked for a while, then decided to enter one of the smaller conduits. He passed several and finally selected one through which ran a bunch of small pipes. He sighed and flicked his cigarette away, hearing a fleeting hiss as it struck the grey current. He jammed himself into the opening and went forward on his knees through the muck. There came to his nostrils a scent of something that resembled gas. He felt a vacant space before him and wondered how far down was the drop. He swung himself outward onto the rusty pipes by his hands and lowered himself down slowly into a pool of cold sludge. He sneezed; he struck a match; the place was surrounded by walls of mud. He took his crowbar and hacked away at the damp clay enclosing the pipes. He soon made a hole big enough to admit his body and then he tunneled forward through soft earth for about three feet. A brick wall confronted him and he pried enough bricks loose—lying flat on his stomach in wet mud—to crawl forward again; he pushed into what seemed an abandoned basement. All about him was the reeking odor of rot. He was startled to detect faint sounds of voices above him, nearing and receding. Was he in danger? He looked up and saw a ceiling made of planks criss-crossed by two-by-four beams of wood. To his right a pale column of daylight fell from a source he could not see.

He saw rickety steps mounting upward and heard the heels of people tapping past along a sidewalk. Carefully he went up to a door and peered through the keyhole and saw a glass window at the front; a wan sun shone in the street; people passed to and fro and now and then a fragment of laughter or the whir of a speeding auto came to him. He squinted closer and saw yards of mosquito netting covering piles of pears, lemons, oranges, bananas, peaches, and plums. His mouth watered. Was anyone in the place? Naw; they would've heard me by now. . . . He pried off the lock and stepped inside. Across the front window, in reverse letters, was: NICK'S FRUITS. . . . He laughed, picked up a big, ripe, yellow pear and bit into it; juice squirted out of the corners of his mouth. A pleasant tingling set up in his throat as his saliva glands reacted to the acid of the pear. He ate three pears, then gobbled two bananas, and made away with several oranges, taking a big bite out of the tops and holding them to his mouth and squeezing them as he sucked the juice.

He found a faucet, turned it, and pursed his lips under the stream until his stomach seemed about to burst. He straightened and belched, feeling satisfied for the first time since he had been underground. He sat upon the floor and rolled and lit a cigarette, his blood-shot eyes squinting against a drifting film of smoke. Sitting, he watched the sky turn red, then purple. Night fell and he lit another cigarette, brooding over the insoluble questions which the experiences of the underground had given him. Restless melancholy made him rise and stand in front of the door; he hovered between the world aboveground and the world underground, pinioned upon the edge of a decision. He wanted to go out, but sober judgment urged him to remain; he spoke aloud in an agonizing voice: "Naw, I can't go out! They'll kill me . . ." Then he did a strange thing; he took out the crowbar and pried the lock loose with one swift twist of the wrist. The door swung outward and through the waning light he saw two people, a white man and a white woman, coming down the sidewalk; he stood immobile in the shadowy doorway and waited for them to pass. But they came directly to the door, paused, confronted him, smiling.

"I want to buy some grapes," the woman said to him.

He stepped back into the store, terrified. The man who accompanied the woman stepped to one side and the woman entered the store.

"You'd better give me a pound of the dark ones," the woman said, pointing.

"Why don't you turn on the light in here?" the man asked.

"Were you just closing?" the woman asked quickly.

"Yes, ma'am," he stammered. For a moment he did not breathe; then he stammered again: "Yes, ma'am."

At that moment the street lamps came on, throwing illumination into the store. He moved dreamily to a counter and lifted up a huge bunch of grapes and held them toward the woman.

"That's fine," the woman said. "But that's more than a pound, isn't it?"

He did not answer; he still held the grapes in the air before her eyes. He came to himself and saw that the man was staring at him intently.

"Put them in a bag for me," the woman said, fumbling in her purse.

He looked about and saw a pile of paper bags under a narrow ledge; he opened one and put the grapes into it.

"Thanks," said the woman, placing a dime in his hands.

The man came closer and stared at his face.

"Where's Nick?" the man asked. "At supper?"

"Yes, sir," he answered.

They left and he stood in the doorway like an image of stone. He burst out laughing and flung the dime to the floor. He stepped outside into the warm, sultry air and breathed it deeply into his lungs. He looked up and saw a few shy stars and he trembled with fear and gladness. The look of the world was beautiful, yet, under the surface of this beguiling drapery he felt the lurking threat. The kinder the aspect of things were, the more he recoiled. A white man passed and glanced at him and he grew afraid. After the man had vanished, he took a few steps along the pavement toward an unattended newsstand and looked at a stack of papers. He saw a headline:

HUNT BLACK WHO COMMITTED
DOUBLE MURDER

He felt that someone was stripping off his clothing and his nakedness was being revealed. He looked about wildly and snatched a newspaper from the pile and tucked it under his arm and walked uneasily back to the door. He shuddered. Yes, the warm summer evening, though starry, clean, exciting, was thick with death. Wet with fear, he went quickly to the rear of the store and descended the steps and at once, as soon as the darkness and silence of the underground had cast its cloak about him, he felt at home. Lingering in his mind was the image of the street with its soft lights and he loathed it with every drop of his blood. They ain't going to get me, he resolved bitterly. He sighed, feeling that a grave issue had been settled. He climbed into his hole and waded across the pool of sludge and slithered through the long tunnel of wet clay and stood again in the inky darkness of the sewer with the friendly, grey water churning at his feet. Yet, he knew deep down in him that the ultimate decision was still to come, for, though the underground claimed him, it rejected him. The conviction that he could not stay slept uneasily in his heart. . . .

IX

By the hazy light of a manhole cover, he unrolled the newspaper and read the news of his being wanted and chased; he had committed a double murder, they said, a horrible murder, and should die. In big, black type was the assertion that he had admitted his guilt. But I didn't do it! he exclaimed with an inward groan. The match flame went to darkness and he balled the paper in violent anger and ripped it to shreds and cast the bits onto the surface of the grey water with a sweeping gesture of unappeasable protest.

He turned and made his way slowly to the cave. He sat upon the chest and he knew that he was trapped. He could not stay here and he could not go out. He reached for a cigarette and lit it; the flame blazed and lit the green-papered walls to militant distinctness; the purple sheen on the gun barrel trembled; the meat cleaver brooded with its eloquent stains of blood; the mound of silver and copper coins smoldered angrily; the diamonds winked at him from the floor; and the gold watches mocked him with their incessant ticking, crowning time the king of consciousness, defining the limits of living. The match blaze died and darkness claimed the room. Yes, sooner or later, he would have to go into that obscene sunshine and say something somehow to somebody about all of this. He sat brooding in the dark.

The sound of singing coming from beyond the wall made him cock his head. Oh, they woke me up. . . . Yeah, I can look at 'em, he thought. He hoisted himself and lay stretched atop the pipes and brought his face to the narrow slit; men and women stood here and there between pews. A song ended and a young black girl tossed back her head and closed her eyes and broke plaintively into another hymn:

> *Glad, glad, glad, oh, so glad*
> *I got Jesus in my soul . . .*

Those few words were all the girl sang, but what her words did not say, her emotions said as she repeated the lines, varying the mood and tempo, making her tone express meanings which her mind could not formulate. Another woman rose and melted her voice with that of the girl, and then an old man rose and joined the two women. Soon the entire church was singing:

> Glad, glad, glad, oh, so glad
> I got Jesus in my soul . . .

The song lashed him to impotent fury. Those people were pleading *guilty*, wallowing sensually in their despair. He gritted his teeth. How could one ever get used to this thing? Overcome with wonder, he felt suddenly that he *knew*, that he had snared the secret! *Guilt!* That was it! Insight became sight and he knew that they thought that they were guilty of something they had not done and they had to die. The song beat on:

> Glad, glad, glad, oh, so glad
> I got Jesus in my soul . . .

They feel they've done something wrong, he whispered in the lyrical dark. He felt that their search for a happiness they could never find made them feel that they had committed a great wrong which they could not remember or understand. He was now in possession of the feeling that gripped him when he had first listened to the singing. It came to him in a series of questions: Why was this sense of guilt so seemingly innate, so easy to come by, to think, to feel, so verily physical? It seemed that when one felt this guilt one was but retracing in one's living a faint pattern designed long before; it seemed that one was trying to remember a gigantic shock that had left an impression upon one's body which one could not forget, but which had been almost forgotten by the conscious mind, creating in one a state of external anxiety.

The singing surged:

> *Glad, glad, glad, oh, so glad*
> *I got Jesus in my soul . . .*

He got down from the pipes and stood; he had to tear himself away from this. Then, with the springy movement of a runner poised waiting for the crack of the pistol, he bolted from the spot and collided brutally with the green-papered wall. The spell was broken. He blinked and glared about in the darkness.

He crawled back through the dark tunnel to the sewer and stood once more in the current, breathing heavily; the physical exertion afforded him respite from tension. Well, what was there left for him to do? He did not know. But he knew that if he stood here until he made up his mind, he would never move. He scampered over the coal pile and through the hole and stood again in the basement of the building where he had stolen the money. He mounted the box beneath the window and hoisted himself up into the areaway. He climbed the rain pipe and squinted through the two-inch opening. He saw the steel safe and heard excited voices. What was going on? A man wearing a blue suit passed between him and the safe. He strained forward. Yes, the man looked familiar. Then the man turned and he saw a star on his chest. *Lawson!* He understood now; they had discovered the robbery. His heart pounded as he saw Lawson's white finger shaking, pointing to someone.

"Nobody but you had the combination to this safe!" Lawson's voice boomed.

There was a mumbled reply which he could not hear. He felt sorry for the man who was being accused as he had once been accused of a crime he had not committed. Perhaps he should tear all of the money off the walls and dump it in the basement and send them a note telling them where to look for it? Naw, he said softly. What good would that do? The man was guilty; he had been stealing money. Although the man was not guilty of the crime of which he was now being accused, he was guilty; he had always been guilty. He nodded understandingly, feeling that this unfounded accusation was merely serving to bring to the man's attention, for the first time in his life, the secret of his existence. Now he could see nothing; Lawson had gone beyond the line of his vision. At times Lawson shouted:

"Shut up! Shut up!"

He heard a soft whimpering sound so poignantly that it seemed that the accused man was standing at his shoulder, weeping. Then he saw the blonde-haired, blue-eyed white girl standing in the middle of the floor nervously knotting a handkerchief in her fingers and staring distractedly. There was one time when she looked up and her eyes were wide and grief-stricken and held an expression that made him think that she had seen him. He trembled. The girl looked down. No, she had not seen him. She left the room and then for the first time he saw the guilty man; he was tall, lean, young, with a straight-forward, clean-shaven face. There were lines about his mouth and eyes that denoted strain.

He stiffened and caught his breath as he watched the man glance over his shoulder and go quickly to a desk and open a drawer and take out a pistol. The man came slowly to the center of the room and stood looking down at the floor, gun in hand; then he bit his lips and a tiny line of blood etched its way down a corner of his chin. He lifted the gun and placed the barrel at his temple and there was a loud report and the man's head jerked violently; he fell forward on his face as though a ton of force had struck him and he lay like a log; in the same instant the gun skidded along the surface of the floor and clattered to a stop against a wall, its blue metal glinting triumphantly.

Lawson came running into the room, gun in hand; he saw the sprawled figure, knelt, and rolled the body over. A scarlet hole gaped in the man's temple and on the floor one hand lay in a widening pool of blood. Lawson went to the washroom and returned with a white towel which he spread over the man's face. Several people were now standing about, looking down at the dead man; among them was the blonde-haired, blue-eyed girl pressing a handkerchief against her mouth and staring with transfixed eyes.

He heaved a sigh and got down from the rain pipe and crawled back into the basement. The dead man was already completely gone from his mind and he was bent toward other goals. Again he felt that he was almost ready to leave the underground; but not quite. He was searching for other prods to confirm his feelings, waiting for his feelings to speak to him in still more unmistakable terms.

X

He re-entered the sewer and came to the opening into which he had crawled to get the rings and watches and diamonds. What's happening in there? he wondered. He climbed into the opening and lay flat on his back and pulled himself forward by lifting his body as he crawled hand over hand along the pipe. Would his returning to look be dangerous? Perhaps they would be so engaged in trying to find the burglar that they would not think of looking for a hole in the storage locker. He paused; it was so quiet that he could hear his own breathing and more than anything else that puzzled him. He had expected to hear sounds of commotion, the same tumult of voices that he had heard in the office of the real estate company when it was discovered that the money was missing from the safe. Was this a trap? Was someone waiting for him? He peered ahead and all was darkness. What had become of the night watchman? The watchman's being wrongly accused might serve to lift him into a higher state of awareness. That was his whole attitude toward the plight of the watchman; he could no longer feel remorse.

His muscles stiffened and he gripped the pipe. He heard sounds of footsteps, steady, continuous. Where were they? When he reached the hole he caught a glimpse of light; he had to be very careful now. Footsteps sounded; bomp . . . bomp . . .

bomp . . . bomp. . . . Mouse-like, he crawled out of the hole and peeped through the door of the locker and he was stunned by the guilty familiarity of what he saw. Framed before him at the far end of the basement in a tableau of bright daylight was a vision that made him want to rush forward and perform some deed of expiation. He stared at two men, both of whom he knew at once. Sitting in a chair, naked to his waist, was the night watchman over whose sleeping body he had stood at some time in the recent past. Walking to and fro in front of the watchman was Murphy, in his shirt sleeves, a cigarette jutting obliquely from his mouth, a gun swinging from his hip. The white flesh of the watchman's body was mottled with crimson welts.

He's trying to make that man tell something he don't know, he whispered. Then he was looking not at Murphy torturing the man, but a moving picture. All of this was unreal; someone was depicting this scene for his benefit so that he could react to it and fathom its meaning. The night watchman sat with his hands upon his knees, his head sagging forward, his face swollen and dirty, his eyes half closed; it seemed that at any moment his body would slump to the floor. Murphy paused, turned, just as the three policemen had paused and turned to him time and again when he had sat in the room at the police station.

"Ready to tell me about it, Thompson?" Murphy asked. "Want to talk now? Was it an inside job?"

The night watchman said nothing. Then he lifted his head and spoke in a sing-song voice:

"I've told you all I know . . ."

Murphy bent forward and slapped the night watchman across the mouth.

"Come clean, you bastard!"

Like a huge, overgrown child, the watchman repeated mechanically:

"I've told you all I know . . ."

Murphy went to the back of the watchman's chair and jerked it from under him; the dazed watchman pitched forward upon his face. He, too, had been dumped upon the floor, so closely did he identify himself with the watchman; but it was not an identification stemming from pity; no, he felt that this was somehow a good thing; it would awaken the watchman from his long sleep of death, would let him see, through the harsh condemnation of Murphy, more of the hidden landscape than he would ever see in any other way.

"Get up!" Murphy snapped.

The watchman pulled slowly to his feet and sat his limp body unsteadily in the chair.

"Now, are you going to talk?" Murphy asked.

As he gripped the iron pipe and stared in horror at the proceedings, he wanted to scream to Murphy that the man was innocent, that the man did not know anything, that no one knew anything, that no man could explain his innocent guilt. He wanted to yell: *He's innocent! I'm innocent! We're all innocent!* The thoughts came to him so hard that he thought he had actually yelled them out; but he had not spoken; his teeth were clenched. The words had screamed inside of him, hot words trying to burst through a tight wall. And again he was overwhelmed with that inescapable emotion that always cut down to the foundations of life here in the underground, that emotion that told him that, though he were innocent, he was guilty; though blameless, he was accused; though living, he must die; though possessing faculties of dignity, he must live a life of shame; though existing in a seemingly reasonable world, he must die a certainly reasonless death.

Watching the man who was being accused, staring at Murphy who marched to and fro, he felt hot tears running down his cheeks. He had seen enough; there was nothing he could do. Mole-like, he wriggled through the hole to the sewer, then plodded on, still feeling that he had to perform some act which he did not understand. He made his way back to the cave and crawled through the holes into the basement of the undertaking establishment. Despite the fact that the mere thought of doing so revolted him, he wanted to go back in again and look, as though to look were a compulsion. Once more he smelt the odor of strange chemicals; once again he groped for the wooden steps with his wet feet and mounted to the top on tiptoe and saw the keyhole. Squinting into the yellow room, he saw not the nude, black body of a man, but the nude, brown body of a woman. He felt that ever since he had gone from here there had been an endless succession of such bodies lying there, being made ready for burial and taken away only to be replaced quickly by others. He had the feeling that men and women were standing in long lines outside of the undertaker's door, waiting their turn to lie upon the white table. He felt sorry for the woman; he knew that she had died expecting to reap a rich harvest of eternal happiness and there was for her now only this coldness and endless time. He felt that, though she was dead, she was somehow still alive, standing over her waxen body at the white table, looking with wet eyes of sorrow upon herself, wringing her hands in grief at her shameful end. *Why? Why?* the woman whispered as she wept. Then he was startled to hear the clear, innocent, piping voice of a child wailing: *Mama, I want a piece of bread. . . . Please, mama. . . .* He whirled from the keyhole and struggled through the opening in the wall and stood again in the cave. Just a little more and he would be through; just a little more and he would be ready to leave the underground. . . .

Restless, he crawled back into another basement; he saw steps leading upward and he became excited by their familiar aspect. Had he gone up those steps? Yes, beyond that door was the room from which he had taken the radio. He mounted the steps and eased the door open and heard sounds of angry voices. He identified the voices racially; the fact that there were black voices and white voices enabled him to understand the suffering and shame and humiliation that was being undergone. The voices came from a door in front of him. Yeah, Johnson's in there, he mumbled.

"Come on, boy! What did you do with the radio?"

"Mister, I ain't stole no radio! I ain't *seen* no radio!"

He heard a thudding sound and imagined a black boy being struck violently.

"What did you do with that radio, you black bastard?"

"I ain't took no radio! I got my own radio at home," the black boy's voice rose hysterically. "You can go to my house and look . . ."

"What in hell do I want to go to your goddamn house for?"

There came to his ears the sound of another blow. He was coiled, tense; he wanted to leap through the narrow hole and across the dark of the basement and up the stairs and rescue the boy, telling him: *Yeah, tell 'im you stole the radio, even if you didn't. Tell 'im you're guilty. . . . Don't you know you're guilty?* And then he wanted to turn to Johnson and say: *Sure, you're guilty, too. Why do you want to beat this innocent boy?* He could not stand it anymore; in frantic haste he replaced the bricks and rushed back into the sewer. A fever burned in his loins with a steadiness that would not allow him to remain still. He pushed through the leaden water with eyes staring as though propped open by invisible hands, as though they had become lidless.

[Part Three]

EVERY MOVE he made now was informed with a marvelous precision; his entire muscular system seemed reinforced from a reservoir of unlimited energy. He looked up; above him was a manhole cover and running up the sides of the sewer wall were several projecting steel hooks that formed a sort of ladder. He caught hold and lifted his body and put his shoulder to the cover and moved it an inch. There came to him a crash of sound and he looked into a hot glare of sunshine through which moved blurred shapes. Fear scalded him and he dropped back into the sewer's pallid current and stood paralyzed in the shadows. A heavy car rumbled past overhead, warning him to remain in this world of dark light, jarring the steel manhole cover back into place with an imperious clang. He stood in a network of tiny poles of light flowing down from above him.

At that moment he did not really know how much fear he felt, for fear had claimed him completely; and yet it was not a fear of the policemen or the autos or the people, but a hot panic at the actions he felt he would perform if he went out into that sunshine. He stood between that terrifying world of life-in-death above him and this dark world that was death-in-life here in the underground. His mind said no; his body said yes. Torn, he knew he had to meet this thing. A low whine of impatience broke from his lips. He climbed upward again and heard the loud honking of auto horns; now and then he caught the faint snatches of human voices. He clung to the steel prongs rigidly, like a frantic cat clutching a piece of cloth; then he heaved his shoulder against the manhole cover and it slid off completely and for a moment his eyes were drowned in the terror of yellow sunshine and he stood in a deeper darkness than he had ever known during the long days he had lived underground.

Half out of the hole, he blinked, regaining enough sight to make out meaningful forms. A strange thing was happening: Traffic stopped, but no one rushed forward to challenge him. He had imagined his emergence as a desperate tussle with men who wanted to cart him off to be killed; instead, the flow of life froze about him. He pushed the cover aside, crawled out, stood up, swaying a little in a world so fragile that he expected it to collapse and drop him into some deep void. But nobody seemed to pay any attention to him. Cars were swerving slowly out of their paths to avoid the gaping black manhole. A raucous voice yelled:

"Why in hell don't you put up a red light, dummy?"

He understood; these people thought he was a workman. He walked toward the sidewalk.

"Look where you're going, nigger!"

"That's right! Stay there and get killed!"

"You blind, nigger?"

"Go home and sleep your drunk off!"

He saw a policeman standing on the corner, looking in the

opposite direction. Where was he? Was this real? He did not know. He wanted to look around to get his bearings, but he felt that something awful would happen if he did. He walked idly into the spacious doorway of a store that sold men's suits and saw his reflection in a long mirror: His high cheekbones protruded from a hairy black face; his greasy cap perched askew upon his head and his red eyes were sunken and glared oddly. His clothing was caked with damp mud and hung loosely; his hands were gummed with a black stickiness and the nails had grown long and claw-like. He threw back his head and laughed so loud that passersby stopped and stared.

He walked on, not in any given direction. He looked up and saw a street sign that read: COURT STREET—HARTSDALE AVENUE. He knew where he was. In his mind he saw an image of the police station and at once he turned and walked north. Yeah, that's where I'm going, he said aloud as though reminding himself of something temporarily forgotten. He would go to the station, clear up everything, make a statement. What statement? He did not know. *He* was the statement, and since it was all so clear to him, surely he would, in one way or another, make it clear to others.

He passed a newsstand and tarried, expecting to see his picture and his name, but strangely, there was nothing about him on the front page; maybe it was on another page? He opened a paper and turned the pages and saw nothing. He was bewildered; then he dismissed the whole thing. What did it matter after all? Even if he had been mentioned, it would not alter things for him.

He came to the corner of Hartsdale Avenue and turned

westward. Yeah, there's the police station. . . . A policeman came down the steps and walked toward him and passed without a glance. Another policeman came out and walked westward, away from him. He mounted the stone steps and there was a smile about the grimy corners of his mouth. He went through the door and paused in a hallway where several policemen were standing, talking, smoking. One turned to him.

"What do you want, boy?"

He looked at the policeman and laughed.

"What in hell you laughing about?" the policeman asked.

He stopped laughing and stared. He was full of what he wanted to say, but he could not say it. He groped for words, but none came. One of the policemen walked over and reached out with his right hand and tugged at his sleeve.

"You want the Desk Sergeant?"

"Yes, sir," he said; then quickly: "No, sir."

"Well, make up your mind, now."

Four policemen grouped themselves about him and stared hard into his eyes. He cleared his throat, smiled and said quietly:

"I'm looking for the men . . ."

"What men?"

Peculiarly, at that moment he could not remember the names of the three policemen. He saw the cave, the money on the walls, the gun, the cartridges, the cleaver, the diamonds, the watches, and the rings. . . . How could he say it? There was a vast distance between what he felt and these men.

"What men?" the policeman repeated.

"Those men who picked me up and brought me here," he

mumbled in a tone so low that the policemen leaned forward to hear him.

"What?"

"The men, mister. They brought me here."

"When?"

His mind flew back over the blur of time lived in the underground blackness. When had he gone down? He had no notion whatever of how much time had elapsed. The intensity of what had occurred could not have happened, his feelings told him, within a short space; yet his mind told him that the time must have been short. Nervously, he rubbed his hands across his eyes. Then he knitted his brows and spoke like a child relating a dimly remembered dream.

"It was a long time ago. I ran away . . . They beat me . . . I was scared . . . And I saw a man stealing money . . ." Just as he was warming to his story, he saw a policeman raise a finger to his head and make a derisive circle.

"Nuts," the policeman whispered.

"Do you know what this place is, boy?" one policeman asked. "Can't you remember?"

"The police station," he answered sturdily.

"Well, who do you want to see?"

"The men," he said again, feeling that surely they knew the men. They were playing with him. "You know the men," he said in a hurt tone.

"Where do you live?" one of the policemen asked.

He stared. What did that matter? It had been so long ago that he felt it was foolish even to try to remember. For an instant he forgot the policemen and the old mood that dominated his life underground surged back; he leaned forward and spoke eagerly.

"I signed the paper, then I run off. Now, I'm back . . ."

"Did you run off from an *institution*, boy?" one of the policemen asked.

He blinked, shaking his head.

"No, sir," he said, smiling. "I come out from under the ground." Then he added as though it were an afterthought: "I pushed off the manhole cover and climbed out . . ."

"Send 'im to the psycho," one of the policemen said with a wry smile.

"You're nuts, ain't you, boy?" one policeman asked, placing a friendly arm about his shoulders.

He smiled at them all.

"Maybe he's a Fifth Columnist!" a policeman shouted.

There was laughter and, despite his anxiety, he joined in. But the laughter went on so long that it irked him and his face grew solemn.

"I got to find those men," he mumbled in mild protest.

"Did they wear white uniforms?" one asked.

He stared with wide eyes, then backed away and pointed his finger at them, as though making a great discovery.

"They were men like you-all," he exclaimed.

"We're policemen. This is a police station. Now, which one of these policemen do you want to see?"

"Oh, yes, sir. I know 'em," he said, as though they had told him that he would not know them if he saw them. "They picked me up . . ."

"Say, boy, what you been drinking?"

"I got some water in the basement," he said simply.

An elderly, white-haired policeman came to him and caught hold of his arm.

"Look, son. Try and think. Where did those men pick you up?"

He knitted his brows in an effort to remember. Had he been back in the labyrinth of the sewers, he could have easily remembered where they had picked him up; but now he was blank inside. The policemen stood before him demanding logical answers, and he could no longer think with his mind; he thought with his feelings and no words came.

"Why did they pick you up?" one of the men asked.

"I was guilty," he stammered. "No, sir. Not then, I wasn't. I mean, mister . . ."

"Aw, come on. Talk sense! Now, where did they pick you up?"

He felt challenged and a sense of duty toward himself made him forget the policemen, and he began reconstructing the events of the past in reverse: He had been standing in that vestibule; and, yes, he had just gone into the vestibule to get out of the rain; and he had been walking along the street when it had begun raining; yes, he had just leaped out of that hospital window to escape those men who had brought him to the police station and beat him and made him sign a paper and he had said: *Please, get in touch with Mrs. Wooten.* . . .

"Oh, yes, sir," he said brightly, smiling, happy that he had recalled it. "I was coming from Mrs. Wooten's . . ."

"Where does she live?"

"Next door to Mrs. Peabody, that place where them folks was . . ."

"That's Lawson's beat," one of the policemen said.

"Where's Lawson?" the elderly man asked.

"Upstairs in the swing-room," someone answered.

"Take 'im up, Sam, and see," a policeman said.

"Okay. Come on, son," the elderly man said.

The old man took hold of his arm, led him up a flight of stairs, down a hallway, and opened a door.

"Lawson!" the old man called.

"What?" a gruff voice answered.

"Someone to see you. A boy . . ."

"What does he want?"

The elderly man caught his arm and pushed him forward into the room.

He stared, his heart barely beating. Before him were the three policemen: Lawson, Johnson, and Murphy. They were seated about a table, playing cards. The air was blue with smoke and sunshine poured through a high window, lighting up fantastic smoke-shapes. Murphy was first to look up; his face was heavy and tired and a cigarette drooped from his mouth. His lips parted in amazement.

"Lawson!" Murphy exclaimed, holding both of his hands tightly about a few cards.

"Looking for me?" Lawson mumbled, sorting his cards. "For what?"

"Don't you-all remember me?" he blurted breathlessly.

He ran to the center of the room and halted about two

feet from the table. All three of the policemen were looking steadily at him now. Lawson leaped to his feet.

"Where in hell've you been?" Lawson demanded tensely.

"Lawson, do you know who he is?" asked the elderly man who had brought him.

"Hunh? Oh, yes," Lawson stammered. "I'll handle this." The elderly man left and Lawson rushed across the room and closed the door and turned the key in the lock. "Come here, boy," Lawson said in clipped, cold tones as he came back to the table.

He did not move. He looked at all three of them. Yes, he had to tell them.

"Can't you hear?" Lawson barked at him.

Still he did not reply. Johnson and Murphy rose and now all three of them were staring at him. He smiled at them.

"Where did you go, boy?" Lawson asked in a quieter tone.

"I went . . . I . . . I went underground . . ."

"*What*?" Lawson screwed up his eyes and twisted his mouth.

"I went underground," he repeated simply.

"He looks batty to me," Murphy said.

"You've been hiding, hunh?" Lawson asked in a tone that denoted that he had ignored his previous answer.

"No, sir."

The room was silent for a long moment.

"Why in hell did you come back?" Lawson asked.

"I . . . I just didn't want to run away no more," he said. "I'm all right now, mister." He paused; the men's attitude puzzled him. In panic he wondered if they were *indifferent*! That was it! They did not care what he said; they thought that they knew what he was about to say! They were not afraid or curious! He tightened inside. Yes, they were waiting for him to speak and then they would laugh at him! He had to rescue himself from this bog; he had to force the reality of himself upon them. "I'll sign some more papers," he told them, leaning forward and speaking with all the fervor he could muster. "I'm guilty . . ."

"I'll be damned," Lawson muttered. "You're off your nut." With slightly shaking fingers he lit a cigarette. "Sit down, boy."

He did not move. His lips trembled. His perceptions seemed out of focus; these men did not seem to be the same men of whom he had thought so constantly while underground. Why? Sprawling within him were the ideas he wanted to shout, but the solid presence of these men seemed to make it impossible for his ideas and feelings to assume the form of words. In a dim way he had the feeling that these men were a part of himself, stifling upon his emotions.

"Listen here, boy," Murphy said uneasily, "let me tell you something for your own goddamn good, see? We don't want you. You are free, free as air. Go home to your wife and son and forget about it. It *was* a son she had, didn't you know? We don't want you to sign anything . . . It was all a mistake, see? We caught the guy who killed Mr. and Mrs. Peabody. He wasn't a colored boy at all . . . He was an Eyetalian . . ."

"Shut up!" Lawson screamed at Murphy. "Have you no sense?"

The room was quiet. Why were they fussing? His coming back to surrender ought to have established peace.

"I'm back now," he whispered in a childlike tone. "I'm guilty . . ."

Lawson puffed at his cigarette, eyeing him coldly.

"Guilty of what?" Lawson asked.

"I was down in the basement," he began after taking a deep breath; he spoke as though repeating a lesson learned by heart; "and I went into a movie . . ." His voice trailed off. No, he was getting ahead of his story. He ought to tell them first about the people singing in the church, but what words could he use? He looked at them appealingly; he would find words to tell about the church later. "I went into a shop and stole a lot of money, a whole sackful of money. And I stole some diamonds and rings and watches and a gun and a radio." As he talked his eyes held a vacant look; he saw before him the dirt room and he mentioned the objects in it as he saw them. "And I stole a meat cleaver and a tool chest and a man's lunch . . . But I didn't steal 'em to use 'em. They're down there now. I'll give 'em all back. I just took 'em and pasted the hundred-dollar bills on the wall . . ."

"What wall?" Lawson asked with puzzled eyes.

"The wall of the cave," he said smiling. "And I hung up the rings and I put the diamonds on the dirt floor and stomped 'em into the ground." He paused, trying to tell from the expressions on their faces just how much they were understanding of what he was saying. Their eyes were hard, cold, disbelieving. Panic was in him again.

"*What* are you talking about, boy?" Lawson demanded.

Lawson reached out with his open palm and slapped him hard across the face. He fell back and into a chair. He tried to rise but Murphy pushed him back into a sitting posture.

"Where've you been?" Murphy demanded.

"Underground, sir," he answered again, his eyes wide and intent upon their faces.

"Look, boy, you didn't have to come back here," Johnson said.

"Goddammit, I told you guys to quit talking to him like that!" Lawson shouted in a wild rage. "We can't let this fool go! He acts crazy, but that may be a stunt."

The three men looked at one another in silence. Then all three of them came and stood over his chair. Helpless, he looked up at them, waiting for their judgment, smiling, ultimately confident.

"Well," Lawson said at last, rubbing his chin, "what're we going to do with 'im?"

"We've got to get 'im out of here," Murphy said.

Their faces were deadly serious now and he interpreted that to mean that they were going to make up their minds about him, that soon they were going to hear him out, to believe him and let him show them what he had seen.

"We can't let 'im go blabbering," Lawson said. He turned to Murphy. "Where's that paper he signed?"

"What paper?" Murphy asked.

"The *confession*, fool!" Lawson exploded in exasperation.

"Oh, I got it here in my pocket," Murphy said.

Murphy pulled out his billfold and extracted a crumpled piece of paper. At once he recognized it as the paper he had signed.

"Yes, sir, mister!" he exclaimed, rising and eagerly stretching forth his hand, "that's the paper I signed . . ."

Lawson slapped him again and he would have toppled over had his chair not struck the wall behind him. Lawson scratched a match and held the paper over the flame. There was silence in the room as the paper burned down to Lawson's fingertips.

"You see, boy," Lawson began soothingly, "I'm burning this paper, see? You didn't sign anything. It was all a bad dream, see?" Lawson came close to him with the blackened ashes cupped in the palm of his hand. "You don't remember a thing about this, do you, boy?"

He stared, thunderstruck. His lips moved soundlessly. Were they joking with him? They had burnt up the one thing that had given a meaning to his life! The dim light of the underground was fleeing and the terrible darkness of day stood before him.

"Oh, yes, sir," he said hopefully, laughing despite the bloody crack in his lip. "That was the paper I signed. But how come you-all burn it up?" he asked hysterically.

"I told you that paper didn't mean anything!" Lawson yelled.

"Don't you-all be scared of me," he pleaded, noticing their fear and uneasiness. "And I'll sign another paper for you." He lowered his head and began to whimper. "I'll show you everything I did . . ."

"What's your game, boy?" Johnson asked, taking hold of his shoulders. "What do you want? What're you trying to find out? Come on, tell us who sent you back here . . ."

"Nobody sent me here," he sobbed. "I came by myself . . . I just want to show you the room . . ."

"He's plumb bats," Murphy said.

"Let's ship 'im to the psycho," Johnson said.

"Naw, naw," Lawson said. "He's playing a game and I wish to God I knew what it was . . ."

He sensed their uncertainty and felt that he could not make them understand.

"I'm guilty, mister! I saw it all," he told them with nervous excitement. He rose from the chair, shaking with hysteria. "And I saw the man when he blew his brains out because you accused him of stealing that money . . . But he didn't steal it. I took it . . . And I saw you slapping the night watchman trying to make 'im tell about them diamonds and rings and watches . . ."

Tigerishly Lawson grabbed his collar and lifted him bodily from the chair.

"*Who told you about that?*"

"Look, now, Lawson," Johnson said. "Don't get excited. He read about it in the papers. This ain't the first loony to confess to something he didn't do. You burned his confession. Nobody'll believe anything he'd say. Dump 'im in the psycho. There'll be no back-fire. He's off his nut."

"You say he saw it in the newspapers," Lawson said. "Hell, he *couldn't*! It wasn't *printed*!" Lawson pulled forth from his pocket a batch of papers. "I haven't turned in the report."

"Then how did he find out about the bookkeeper?" Murphy asked.

"Get your coats on," Lawson said with resolution.

"Where're we taking 'im?" Murphy asked.

"Come on, I tell you!" Lawson shouted with ragged nerves. This lunatic will queer everything." He turned to the chair as Murphy and Johnson hastily put on their caps and coats and buttoned their guns and cartridge belts about their hips. "Listen, boy, we're going to take you to a good, quiet place where you'll be all right, see? We're going to take care of you, so don't worry . . ."

"Yes, sir. And I'll show you the underground," he told them as he stood eagerly.

"Goddamn!" Lawson muttered as he put on his coat and cap. He buttoned his gun at his side and narrowed his eyes at Johnson and Murphy. "Listen," he said in a voice just above a whisper, "say nothing to nobody, you hear?"

"Sure," Johnson said.

"Okay," Murphy said.

Lawson opened the door and Murphy and Johnson caught hold of his arms and led him out of the room and down the stairs. The hallway was crowded with policemen.

"What did he do, Lawson?" a policeman yelled.

"He's nuts, ain't he, Lawson?" another yelled.

Lawson did not answer; Johnson and Murphy marched him to the car parked at the curb, pushed him into the back seat. Lawson got behind the steering wheel and the car started forward.

"What's up, Lawson?" Murphy asked.

"Listen," Lawson began, "we told the papers that he confessed to the Peabody job, then he escapes. The Wop is caught and we tell the papers that we steered them wrong to trap the real guy, see? Now, this sonofabitch shows up and acts loco. If he goes around squealing about that Peabody job, people'll say *we* framed 'im, see?"

"I'm all right, mister," he said, feeling Murphy's and Johnson's arms locked rigidly in his. "Yeah, I know I'm guilty. Everybody's guilty. I'll show you everything in the underground . . ."

"Sure, sure, son," Murphy said. "Just keep quiet now."

"You see, mister, we're *all* guilty . . ." he began.

"Shut that fool up!" Lawson yelled.

Johnson tapped him across the head with a blackjack; he fell against the seat-cushion, dazed.

"Yes, sir," he mumbled. "That's all right."

"He's a stool trying to get dope for headquarters," Lawson said.

The car shot southward along Hartsdale Avenue, then swung westward at Pine Street and rolled to State Street, then swung south again. It slowed to a stop, then swung around in the middle of the street and headed north again.

"What's up, Lawson?" Johnson demanded.

"We can't take this clown *any*where!" Lawson snarled.

"I'll show you all the holes I dug," he said.

"Shut that coon up!" Lawson snapped.

Murphy and Johnson gripped his arms until he bent forward in pain; the car sped forward. They reached Center Street and turned eastward again and rolled into Jefferson Park. He was confused now; he had been riding for a long time and he wanted the policemen to stop the car so that he could tell them important things. The car went to Jefferson

Street, swung to South Street and headed north again; no word was spoken as Lawson slowed, drove to Court Street, swung eastward and turned onto Jefferson Street and headed north again.

"Say, Lawson!" Murphy yelled. "You're going in circles!"

Lawson was hunched over the steering wheel and did not reply.

"Say, boy, did you see your wife?" Lawson asked.

"My wife?" he repeated, his voice full of vague wonder.

"Where've you *been*? Didn't you go home?"

"No, sir," he said.

Lawson pulled to a stop at the curb.

"Listen, here, boy. Tell us the truth. Haven't you been home?"

"No, sir," he said.

All three of the policemen were staring at him now; he felt that for the first time they were beginning to understand something of what he wanted to tell them.

"Mister, when I looked through all them holes and saw all those people, I loved 'em. I couldn't help it . . ."

"Cut out that crazy talk," Lawson snapped. "Who hid you?"

"Nobody," he said emphatically.

"Maybe he's telling the truth," Johnson ventured.

"All right," Lawson said. "Nobody hid you. Now, tell us where you hid."

"I went underground."

"What goddamn underground cave you talking about?" Lawson shouted.

"I just went . . ." He paused and looked into the street, then pointed to a manhole cover. "I just went down in there and stayed."

"In the *sewer*?" Lawson demanded.

"Yes, sir."

The three policemen looked at one another in silence. Johnson burst into a sudden laugh that ended quickly. Cars swirled by and the air was full of the scent of burning gasoline. Lawson abruptly swung the car off Jefferson Street and drove south along Woodside Avenue. He brought the car to a stop in front of a tall apartment building.

"What're we going to do now?" Johnson asked.

"I'm taking 'im to my place," Lawson said. "We've got to wait until tonight. There's nothing we can do now."

They took him out of the car and led him into the vestibule of the building, then up three flights of steps and into the living room of a large apartment. Murphy and Johnson let go of his arms and he stood uncertainly in the middle of the floor.

"I'll phone the captain that I'm on the trail of something. I'll tell 'im you guys are with me," Lawson said, pulling off his coat and cap. He was about to go out of the door, then turned and said: "Sit down, boy."

"Yes, sir," he said eagerly, but he did not sit. He felt that something would happen soon now.

Lawson left. Murphy and Johnson pulled off their coats and caps and guns and piled them on a chair at the far end of the room, then both of them sat on a sofa and stared at him. Lawson returned.

"It's okay, boys," he said, then walked over to him and stood biting his lips. "Well, boy, looks like you're in for it, don't it?"

"Yes, sir," he answered, looking vaguely around the room, as though annoyed at something.

"You've been gone for three days," Lawson said. "Now, look here, forget all of those wild tales you've been telling and give us the truth. Where did you hide during that time? Who sent you back to us?"

"Nobody, mister. I just went underground, just like I told you," he said. "It started raining and I went down there to get out of the rain . . ."

"So you went down into the sewer just to get out of the rain, hunh?" Murphy asked.

The room rocked with laughter.

"Yes, sir. But after I got down there, I wasn't running anymore."

The policemen shook their heads. Lawson went to a cabinet and took out a bottle of whiskey; he set glasses for Murphy and Johnson. All three of them drank.

"He's nuts," Johnson said. "Come on, Lawson. Let's wash the thing up and take 'im to the psycho."

"I don't know," Lawson said meditatively. "Suppose this Mr. Wooten learns he's there? We can't take that chance . . ."

He felt that he was not explaining himself sufficiently; he sat still, trying to muster all of the symbols that lay sprawling in him. The symbols stood out sharp and clear in his mind, but he could not make them have the meaning for others that he felt they had for him. He felt so helpless that he began to cry.

"He's nuts," Johnson said. "All nuts weep like that."

Murphy crossed the room hurriedly with the bottle of

whiskey in one hand and slapped him across the face with the other.

"Stop that damn raving!"

"No, sir! No, sir! I'm not raving," he sobbed. "I just want to tell you . . ." His voice died and he stared stonily. He rose to his feet again, feeling now that he could speak and tell all, yet not knowing words to convey what he felt. A wild sense of excitement flooded his body and his hands lifted themselves in mid-air, trembling. "Yes, sir. I'm guilty . . . The people in the church know it, but they sing praises for it. Look, you-all, please let me show you . . ." He grew terribly agitated; his lips trembled. He ran to Murphy and grabbed his arm, making him spill whiskey on his shirt. "Come on, I'll show you," he spoke huskily, his eyes seeming to strain in their sockets. "I'll take you to the room where the money is! It's underground . . ."

"Shut up!" Murphy bellowed, slapping him.

He stared at Lawson, then he ran to Lawson, feeling that Lawson alone would understand him, would help him.

"Mister, mister . . ." he whimpered, stretching forth his trembling hands to Lawson. "Please, mister . . . Just let me show you!"

Before he knew it he felt a sharp impact under his chin; darkness covered his eyes. He felt himself being lifted and laid straight out on the sofa. He heard low voices about him and he struggled to rise, but a hard hand caught him and held him. His brain was clearing now. *But I got to show 'em*, he thought desperately. He pulled to a sitting posture and stared with glazed eyes. It had grown much darker. How long had he been out? He did not know.

"Say, boy, will you show us where you went underground?"

"Yes, sir!"

His heart swelled with gratitude. Lawson *believed* him! He rose, glad. He held on to the arm of the sofa, for he was barely able to stand.

"Okay boy. We'll take you down. But you better be telling the truth, you hear? You better show us where you hid."

He clapped his hands with wild joy.

"Yes, sir! I'll show you!" he exclaimed. He had triumphed; he would do what he had felt was compelling him all along. At last he would be free of his burden. "I'll show you everything!"

"Take 'im down," Lawson said.

The three policemen put on their caps and coats and fastened their guns at their hips. Murphy and Johnson took him by his arms and led him down the stairs and into the vestibule. When he reached the street, he saw that it was night and a fine, steady rain was falling.

"Just like when I went down," he told them eagerly.

"What?" Lawson asked.

"The rain," he said, sweeping his arm in wide and generous arcs. The night reminded him of the underground and made him feel at home, as though he were nearing the end of a long journey. He was unshakably confident now. All along he had felt that something like this would happen, and now it was coming true! Now they would see what he had seen; they would hear what he had heard; they would feel what he had felt. He would lead them into the sewer and take the bricks out of the holes he had made. He wanted to make a hymn, to prance about in ecstasy.

"Get into the car, boy," Lawson ordered.

"Yes, sir."

He climbed in and Murphy and Johnson sat to either side of him; Lawson got behind the wheel and started the motor.

"Now, tell me where to go," Lawson said.

"Yes, sir," he said. "To the hospital."

The car rolled slowly; he closed his eyes and he remembered the song he had heard in the church, the song that had wrought him to such a high pitch of terror and pity. He began to sing softly, lolling his head:

> *Glad, glad, glad, oh, so glad*
> *I got Jesus in my soul . . .*

"Stop 'im! He gets on my nerves!" Lawson shouted as the car swished through the rain.

Johnson cuffed him.

"Mister, I ain't done nothing," he mumbled.

"What do you suppose he's suffering from?" Murphy asked.

"Delusions of grandeur, maybe," Lawson said.

"These colored boys sure go off their nuts easy," Murphy commented, nodding sadly.

"It's because they live in a white man's world," Johnson said.

"Say, nigger, what did you eat down here?" Murphy asked, reaching his free hand and touching Johnson in anticipation.

"I ate pears, oranges, bananas, pork chops," he said. "And I had some grapes . . ."

The car filled with laughter.

"And you didn't eat any watermelon?" Lawson asked.

"No, sir," he answered solemnly. "I didn't see any."

The policemen roared harder and louder.

"You're sure a case, boy," Murphy said.

The brakes screeched and the car pulled to a curb.

"All right," Lawson said. "We're at the hospital now. Tell us where to go."

He sat up. Through rain he saw the corner where he had gone down into the manhole.

"Right at the corner . . ." he said, pointing.

The streets, save for a few lamps glowing feebly through the rain, were dark and empty. The car pulled to a stop. He leaned forward and waved his hand.

"Come on. Let's take a look," Lawson said, getting out of the car and looking up and down the rain-filled street.

He was wild to get out of the car now. If he could but show them the things he had seen, then they would feel as he had felt and they in turn would show them to others and those others would feel as they had felt, and soon the whole world would feel the same, everybody in it would be governed by the same impulse of pity.

"Let me show you, mister," he begged with tears in his eyes.

Again Lawson looked up and down the street; no one was in sight. The rain slanted down like black wires across the wind-swept air. Dim yellow squares glowed in the windows of apartment buildings to left and right.

"Take 'im out," Lawson ordered.

Murphy and Johnson opened the door and pushed him forward; he stood trembling in the rain.

"All right, now. Come on and show us," Lawson said.

They freed his arms. Now, he would do it! How amazed

they would be! They would never dream how simple it was until he had shown them! The rain soaked his skin, but he was too happy to notice.

"Show us," Lawson said impatiently.

"Yes, sir."

He stooped and inserted a finger in one of the tiny circles of the manhole cover and tugged, but it did not move. He pulled harder, but he was too weak to budge it.

"Did you really go down in there, boy?" Lawson asked with a twinge of doubt in his voice.

"Yes, sir. Just a minute. I'll show you."

"Help 'im get that damn thing off," Lawson said.

Johnson stepped forward and bent and lifted the cover; it clanged against the wet pavement. The hole gaped blackly.

"I went down in there," he announced with triumphant pride.

Lawson gazed at him for a long time without speaking, then he reached his hand to his holster and drew forth his gun.

"Mister, I got a gun just like that down there," he said, laughing and looking into Lawson's face. "I hung it on the wall."

"Show us how you went down," Lawson said quietly.

"I'll go down first, mister, and then you-all can come after me, hear?" he spoke like a little boy playing a game.

"Sure. We'll come," Lawson said soothingly. "Go on down."

He looked brightly at the three policemen. He turned; then, just as he bent and grasped the rim of the manhole, a siren howled. He straightened and looked about; the three policemen were staring upward.

"Sounds like an air raid alarm," Lawson mumbled.

The policemen seemed to have forgotten him and he was annoyed.

"I'm going down," he said loudly.

Another siren sounded; then another. Soon the rainy air was full of screaming. The policemen stood with lifted faces. A huge bright beam of light shot from the horizon and stabbed the wet sky; another rose and crossed it; within ten seconds the air was full of bright, roving columns of light.

"But, mister," he mumbled, his face lifted too, bewildered at what was happening.

"It's a raid, all right," Lawson breathed.

"Look!" Johnson exclaimed, pointing.

"Planes," Murphy mumbled.

He saw tiny, silver planes were whirling in the beams of light. Then he was aware that the quiet, wet streets were full of people. Tense shouts and screams were heard above the sirens. People rushed past him; half-dressed women with children; men hastily pulling on overcoats; young girls weeping.

"What're we going to do with 'im?" Murphy asked.

"Hunh?" Lawson asked, looking from face to face. Jerking to attention, he bit his lips. "Get on into the hole, boy."

"Yes, sir!" he said.

A sound like thunder came from the west and shook the pavement. Then another, closer. To the east a tongue of red flame licked at the sky.

"Mister!" he exclaimed. "Look . . ."

"Get into the hole!" Lawson barked, his gun pointed at him.

He looked about, then stared in wild joy at the three policemen. Explosions burst about them, jarring the earth.

"Mister, *this is it*! LOOK!"

"Get into the hole!" Lawson yelled.

They didn't believe him! They couldn't see! Lawson's left hand caught his collar, choking him.

"Get into the hole, *now*!"

His muscles tightened with a desire to wrench himself free; then his body relaxed. He sighed, shook his head. They did not understand.

"Yes, sir," he said.

Lawson's fingers left his collar. He bent slowly and placed his hands on the rim of the hole and sat on the edge. He looked up quickly, holding his breath; the jerking pencils of light reminded him of the diamonds on the floor of the cave; the roar of the sirens made him remember the radio; the tall buildings that loomed all about him were like those hundred-dollar bills pasted upon the walls; the distant sound of explosions was like the awful ticking of those golden watches.

"Mister," he pleaded in a whisper.

Naw, it was no use. His feet dangled in watery darkness and he heard the rush of the grey sewer current. He turned and lowered his body and hung by his fingers for a moment, then he went downward on the steel prongs, hand over hand, until he reached the last rung. The three white faces hovered dimly near. He dropped; his feet hit the water and he felt the swift current trying to suck him away. Quickly, he balanced himself and looked back up at the policemen.

"Come on, you-all," he yelled at them, casting his voice about the rustling at his feet.

He saw Lawson raise the gun and point it directly at him

and there was a thunderous report and a streak of fire ripped through his chest. He was hurled into the water, flat on his back. He looked up at the white faces. The grey water was flowing past him, blossoming in white foam about his arms, his legs, his head, his body. His jaw sagged and his mouth gaped open soundlessly. A sharp pain seized his head, a pain that gradually squeezed out the light and let in darkness.

"You-all shot me," he mumbled, breathing hard.

He heard excited voices.

"What you shoot 'im for, Lawson?"

"I had to."

"Why?"

"You've got to shoot his kind. They would wreck things."

He heard a metallic clank; they had replaced the manhole cover, shutting out forever the sound of wind and rain. A muffled roar of a motor came to him and then the heavy swish of a speeding car rumbled overhead. He felt the grey water push his body slowly into the middle of the sewer, turning him about. Feeling still lingered in his limbs and he whispered in amazement: They shot me. . . . He no longer felt the pain of the bullet that had violated his chest, and his mouth was full of thick, bitter water. The current spun him forward. He closed his eyes, a whirling, black object, rushing along in the darkness, veering, tossing with the grey tide, lost in the heart of the earth. . . .

Memories
of My
Grandmother

I HAVE NEVER WRITTEN anything in my life that stemmed more from sheer inspiration, or executed any piece of writing in a deeper feeling of imaginative freedom, or expressed myself in a way that flowed more naturally from my own personal background, reading, experiences, and feelings than *The Man Who Lived Underground*. In fact, I can say that, in the act of writing, for the first time in my life, I reacted as a *whole* to the material before me in an effort to create a simple but meaningful surface of prose. What I mean is this: In all of my other attempts at writing I felt that I was reacting in terms of many partial, limited, and incomplete concepts; but here, in this book, there is only one—expressed in many terms and seen from many points of view, but still *one*—far-reaching, complex, ruling idea-feeling hovering in the background, like the rhythmic beat of the bass in a jazz song, fusing and lending unity and meaning to the images and symbols and movements within the story.

The idea—or, if you prefer to call it, the concept—back of *The Man Who Lived Underground* is half as old as my life and has slept somewhere within my heart since my childhood, awakening now and then to baffle me, to startle me, to amuse me, to fill me with new insight into myself and my environment.

The whole idea is centered around the ardent and volatile religious disposition of my grandmother who died in Chicago in 1934. My grandmother lived her religion day by day and hour by hour; *religion* was her *reality*, the sole meaning in her life. The inconsistencies of her behavior were the subject of much agonizing thought and feeling on my part during at least one-half of my life; indeed, it was my grandmother's interpretation of religion—or perhaps I should say that it was my religious grandmother's interpretation of life—that actually made me decide to run off from home at the age of fifteen.

My mother being an invalid, I lived in my grandmother's house and ate her bread and automatically this dependence obligated me to worship her God. My grandmother practiced the Seventh-Day Adventist religion, a form of religious ritual that encompasses and regulates every moment of living. (I sometimes wonder—even though I've abandoned that faith— if some of my present-day reactions are not derived, in whole or in part, from the extreme and profound effects of the emotional conditioning which I underwent at that period.) A man who worships in the Seventh-Day Adventist Church lives, psychologically, in a burning and continuous moment that never ends: The present is everlasting; the past is telescoped into *now*; there is no future and at any moment Christ may come again and then the anxious tension of time will be no more. . . . Those desiring a more elaborate description of this religion must go to the Seventh-Day Adventist Church itself to learn, for it is something to be felt rather than described.

Often I had thought vaguely of depicting in fictional and symbolic terms the religious disposition of my grandmother and, by doing so, rendering a picture of the inner religious disposition of the American Negro. (Strangely, despite our proud boast that we are a religious people, we have but little literature dealing with religious emotion per se. I exclude such novels as Sinclair Lewis's *Elmer Gantry*; they are satires upon institutional religion and criticisms of much of religious conduct rather than depictions of the living inner springs of religious emotion. After all, it is hard to believe that *every* man who preaches or who goes to church of a Sunday morning is trying to fool somebody! And the descriptions of religious states and reactions by William James, Reinhold Niebuhr, Waldo Frank, et al., are couched in abstract, philosophic rather than concrete, imagistic terms.) What baffled me in my longing to depict the inner structure of my grandmother's religion was my inability to find a suitable form in which it could be couched. I do not mean *literary* form, but form of *action*, a contour of *movement*, a ritualistic scheme whose dynamics would lay bare the inner but not the outer processes of religion. The primitive forms of religious life among the masses of Negroes in America are all too well-known: the shouting, the singing, the moaning, the fainting, and the rolling. . . . I suppose my grandmother indulged in more than her share of these during her lifetime, but these external manifestations, in my opinion, did not indicate the true structure of her religious personality. To me it seemed that the tenets of her religion were illogical if not degrading; the images and symbols of her imagination were largely borrowed from the Old Testament; her actual knowledge of the Bible was limited; her codes of conduct did not add up to anything meaningful; yet, there was *something* elusive but abiding at the core of her personality that she clung to when all else failed and faded, *something* which she preserved even when the styles of religious worship changed. And I was interested in that *something* that made her tick. But I was afraid that if I depicted that *something* in terms of the forms of religious life common among Negroes—forms well-known also to whites—that the attempt would defeat itself, that the reader would be carried away by the local color—à la *The Green Pastures*—and by the peculiar mannerisms and would laugh instead of being enthralled.

My concern with depicting the religious impulses among Negroes—using my grandmother's life as a model—did not in any degree occur to me all at once. The vague desire would well up and subside many times throughout a period of years; but always I'd push the thought aside, feeling that I had not yet found the form of action that would do justice to the principle involved, that would bring out in bold outline the functional pattern of response and reflex that lay at the back of her religious disposition. I did not know that, in my living, many other parallel experiences were happening to me and that at some time in the future—a time when I was not thinking of writing of religion—a spark would ignite a fire of meaning that would fuse them all into one organic concept, a concept that would shed meaning not only upon my grandmother's religion and its relation to me, but would strip the daily mask from the many parallel experiences and show me that at bottom they were all one and the same.

The foremost thing that puzzled me about my grandmother's religious attitude was her callous disregard for the

personal feelings of others and her inability to understand—
and her refusal to even try—anything of the nature of the social relationships obtaining in the world about her. Yet this
callousness toward others, this disdain of things relating to
the life of society as a whole, was united with an abstract,
all-embracing love for humanity. Many times, when the Saturday evening sun was sinking—for Saturday was our Sabbath—
she would call us children together and make us kneel; then
she would pray for the Africans, the Japanese, the Chinese,
and so forth. During weekdays she could be found standing
upon street corners or going from door to door selling religious tracts dealing with the plight of the remote "heathen."
I remember times when I spent the entire night at church,
sitting up and listening to the singing and the preaching and
the praying, fighting sleep, drunk with fatigue; and the next
thing I'd know I would be rubbing my eyes and blinking at the
bright sunshine pouring through stained-glass windows; my
bones would be aching for having slept all night on the hard
church benches.

"While you were sleeping, the Holy Ghost was here," my
grandmother would chide me gently, smiling knowingly.

And I would feel abashed.

Often she prevailed insistently upon me to join church, but
I would always tell her no. When she would ask me what real
objections I had, I would tell her that I had to *see* something
before I would join. She had to accept my explanations, because she had told me that she had not joined until she had
seen something. . . .

One Saturday the elder—the Seventh-Day Adventist call

their pastors *elders* instead of *reverends*, for they feel that only God should be called reverend—preached a sermon about some prophet of the Old Testament who had seen an angel in a vision. I nudged my grandmother and she leaned closer.

"You see, Granny," I whispered, "if I ever saw an angel like that man did, I'd join church."

My grandmother beamed and I wondered vaguely what made her seem so glad. When the service was over my grandmother hurried to the pulpit and spoke with the elder, who, as he listened to my grandmother, looked in my direction. Then I was called to talk with the elder.

"Your grandmother tells me you saw an angel," he said, leveling steady eyes at me.

My mouth gaped open in surprise.

"No, sir," I mumbled.

"You *did* tell me you saw an angel," my grandmother said. "You told me during service . . ."

"No'm," I said hastily, burning with embarrassment, ashamed that so many people were listening. "I told you that *if* I saw one I'd join church . . ."

The elder smiled. My grandmother was angry.

"You *did* tell me!" she said stoutly.

Church members began to laugh.

"Granny, you didn't under*stand*," I said.

My grandmother walked away, hurt. For a week there was coolness between us. Such was the atmosphere in which I spent my most sensitive and formative years. Without hesitation my grandmother would have sacrificed my life if, in doing so, she would have thought that she could have saved

me for eternity. She would have done this because she loved
me; eternity was so real to her that human life had an air of
unreality. Yet, despite this dichotomy, she lived out her daily
actions with a throbbing sincerity that brooked no doubt on
anybody's part. My grandmother would not have dared feed
a tramp who came to her door, but had she dared, after the
tramp had swallowed the last mouthful, she would ask him
what religion he professed and if the tramp's religion differed
from her own, she would have informed him quietly and seriously that he was doomed straight for hell.

My grandmother had deep-set black eyes with over-hang-
ing lids and she had a habit of gazing with a steady, unblinking
stare; in my later life I've always associated her religious ardor
with those never-blinking eyes of hers, eyes that seemed to be
in this world but not *of* this world, eyes that seemed to be contemplating human frailty from some invulnerable position
outside time and space. It may be that she had been religious
so long that the physical structure of her body, her emotional
reactions and reflexes had become somewhat conditioned by
her staunch faith.

Religion as such never deeply interested me; I have never
felt it deeply enough to be swayed to believe, for my sensibilities were too much claimed by the concrete externals of
the world I saw. (At the age of twelve or thirteen I did try to
feel some of the things I'd heard in church, but I never could.)
From the earliest time I can remember, I longed for happiness
here and now, in the form of feeling with the feelings of my
body. Yet, I think I understood with my mind the feelings of
the religious happiness that surrounded me as I grew up. But

I was too sensual for Protestant religion; perhaps some other form of religion might have snared me; I don't know. . . .

What fascinated me about religion was its manifestation in the personalities of others, especially when those manifestations related to me in one way or another and had something to do with my life. For example, when I ran away from home, I was completely baffled by the harsh and implacable attitude which my parents and grandparents held toward me; I felt that somehow they loved me, but in their loving me, they were determined to take me by the throat and lift me to a higher plane of living and, in lifting me, I knew that they would surely strangle me to death.

My grandmother was a rebel, as thorough a rebel as ever lived on this earth; she was at war, ceaselessly, militantly at war with every particle of reality she saw. In her way and according to her light, she strove to transform the world; she fought the world, she attacked it. . . .

I repeat that *The Man Who Lived Underground* did not stem wholly from my memories of my grandmother; without my knowing it, the vast, sprawling symbol of her life sank deep down into me and became associationally united with many other experiences. I shall try to enumerate as many of these experiences as I can remember, but I cannot do so in the exact sequence in which they occurred. For who can tell the boundary lines between experiences? How can one tell when one experience ends and another begins? I remember the objective order in which these experiences happened, but the full significance of each experience did not impress itself upon me as I endured it. In many instances, to my delight or dismay, it was not until years had elapsed that a supposedly new or alien experience would, for one reason or another, doff its stylish clothes and reveal itself as an old experience in disguise. Sometimes these new experiences would be with me for ten years without my ever suspecting that my reaction to them was influenced or controlled by attitudes and conditionings implanted in me by my grandmother.

Now for the enumeration; I shall discuss a paradoxical one first. My grandmother was an enemy of all books save those based upon or derived from the Bible. Whenever I neared home with any books other than those sanctioned by the Seventh-Day Adventist Church school to which I was made to go, I'd push them under my coat and steal to my room and secrete them under the pillow on my bed. Hours later I'd go to look for my books and they would be gone. But I'd never confront my grandmother and ask her where they were; long experience had taught me where they were. I'd go to our wood-burning stove in the kitchen and lift up the lid, and sure enough, there in the black ashes would be what was left of my books. Similarly, no piece of music ever sounded in my home save a hymn. If my grandmother had ever heard me so much as hum a blues song, she would have branded me with whatever she happened to hold in her hands at the moment, be it a broom or an eight-pound, cast-iron skillet.

In contrast to this, my grandmother would pray that I acquire knowledge to get on in the world, in order that I might succeed in supporting myself, and she took great pride in all good reports she heard of my progress in school. But she strove with all of her might to keep any realistic knowledge of the world from me. Her religious faith was so deep and rigid, so uncompromising and fanatic, that it could not manifest itself continuously in daily life. It was capricious, disjointed, brittle, chopped to bits by the daily necessity to live. This was as it had to be, for my grandmother was real, normal, healthy; she had her bodily functions, her temper, her concepts of earthly loyalty; she was married; she loved her husband; she had nine children; she liked to eat, to laugh, to sing, and to play. And yet, through all of this, there spouted spasmodic eruptions of religion, trying desperately by faith to tie all these many earthly—and, to her, *meaningless*—items together into one meaningful and ultimate whole. Another way of expressing it is this: She lived with all of us, yet, psychologically, she hovered somewhere off in space so distantly that things that strike us as having no relationship were merged into an organic blur for her, and things that were united for us were either separate or non-existent for her. To this day, when I look upon my grandmother's life, it seems to me to have been utterly meaningless; yet, to her, I know, her faith tied all of the disparate items of her environment into one meaningful pattern of value. And it was this bringing from *somewhere* else a code of meaning and imposing it upon her home and its life that made life an exasperation to those who lived with her, unless they saw and felt as she did. Always she seemed to be peeping out of Heaven into the world while living in the world.

Now I'll recite an experience in Negro life—an experience that exists on a non-religious plane—that cancels out my grandmother's way of life, or, perhaps I should say, merges with it and becomes, in essence, one. I shall call both of these ways of living—my grandmother's and the one I shall now relate—the "abstract." Perhaps "abstract" is not the right word for it, but I think it will serve the purpose if I define it. What I mean by "abstract" living is simply any way of life that does not derive its meaning and sanction from the context of experience, a way of life that is lived *distantly* from the environment even though it subsists on the environment, a way of living that allows or enables or forces the organism to superimpose judgments and values upon their experiences borrowed from somewhere else.

Perhaps I can best express it in another way. Let's imagine a man cast alone upon a small, unpopulated desert island with, say, a dictaphone, a pair of skates, a million dollars in gold currency, three thousand copies of *The New York Times*, a Chicago telephone directory, a sack of marbles, a doorknob, and a bouquet of red roses. . . . At once we can see that these items have no use or real meaning for him, for they were snatched from the context of another way of life. Yet, let's imagine that our castaway is doomed to live the balance of his natural life with these items and at once we get an inkling of the state of mind of my grandmother (and, incidentally, of the millions of Negroes in America who are surrounded with daily items of civilization to which they cannot react frontally). The only way in which our castaway can get along with these items is to either ignore them altogether or *impose* upon them a meaning alien to them, a meaning which they do not possess intrinsically or in relation to anything else.

And such was what my grandmother did with her religion;

she took concepts from the Old Testament and tagged the items in her environment which did not fit and gave them other names and other meanings. Hence, she ordered me to destroy the first radio I brought into the house. She refused to believe that the music and the voices were coming over the air; she branded it an evil thing of the devil. I doubt seriously if, outside of the daily things which she was forced to use for the sake of keeping life going, she ever linked any of the important segments to each other to make meaning, or if she ever detected any causal relations between the segments. I imagine her world must have looked something like a surrealistic painting. . . . (More on this later.)

I hasten to add that my grandmother's refusal to attempt to see meanings or relationships around her did not flow from any personal weakness on her part. Being a Negro woman, she had more than her share of handicaps to keep the daily, meaningful world in which the majority of people lived from her; and, knowing that such a world was not for her, she gave it up. But, having once surrendered the things of this world, she had perforce to *keep* it from her. She had created a world in which to live and whenever the world before her eyes intruded into her created world, she drove it out with all of the savage vehemence of one who felt that life itself was endangered.

Now for that other experience that cancels out this strange, "abstract" way of living. The Negro blues songs seem to me to approach most nearly in their inner structure and function the quality of my grandmother's living. This may seem odd inasmuch as my grandmother was ardently religious and the blues songs were blatantly secular and the singers of the blues would have certainly loathed my grandmother and my grandmother would have certainly detested them. But in most blues songs the verses have little or no relationship to one another—in the sense that there is practically no causal or logical progression—just as the items of my grandmother's environment were not related. I quote some verses of "Dink's Blues" from *American Ballads and Folk Songs*, collected by John A. Lomax and Alan Lomax:

> *Some folks say dat de worry blues ain' bad,*
> *It's de wors' ol' feelin' I ever had.*
>
> *Git you two three men, so one won't worry you min';*
> *Don' they keep you worried and bothered all de time?*
>
> *I wish to God eas'-boun' train would wreck,*
> *Kill de engineer, break de fireman's neck.*
>
> *I'm gwine to de river, set down on de groun',*
> *Ef de blues overtake me, I'll jump overboard and drown.*
>
> *Ef trouble was money, I'd be a millioneer,*
> *Ef trouble was money, I'd be a millioneer.*
>
> *My chuck grindin' every hole but mine,*
> *My chuck grindin' every hole but mine.*
>
> *Come de big* Kate Adam *wid headlight turn down*
> *de stream,*
> *An' her sidewheel knockin', "Great-God-I-been-redeemed."*

I submit that these verses certainly do not tell a story; they do not progress; in their sequence any one of the verses could be substituted for almost any other and still more verses could be improvised endlessly. Rereading them reveals nothing save an elusive and tenuous strain of melancholy running through them. The items out of which they are built are taken from widely separated sections of the American environment. They are brittle, disjointed; the amount of meaning in any one of them is so slight that one wonders how such verses could have any interest when sung. Yet they have. The meaning, however, does not reside in the verses, but in what is brought to bear upon them.

A black woman, singing the blues, will describe a rainy day, then, suddenly to the same tune and tempo, she will croon of a red pair of shoes; then, without any logical or causal connection, she will sing of how blue and lowdown she feels; the next verse may deal with a horrible murder, the next with a theft, the next with tender love, and so on. This tendency of freely juxtaposing totally unrelated images and symbols and then tying them into some overall concept, mood, feeling, is a trait of Negro thinking and feeling that has always fascinated me. I think it was this part of my grandmother's personality that fascinated me more than anything else. The ability to tie the many floating items of her environment together into one meaningful whole was the *function* of her religious attitude. It seemed indicative of a certain strange *need* on her part.

At the time when I noticed the juxtaposing of unrelated things in the mind and actions of my grandmother and in the Negro blues songs, it never occurred to me that some day, many miles distant from my hometown, I would encounter a "theory" imported from Europe that would enable me to see and understand what those disjointed items meant when they were tied together by the mood, faith, or passion of a personality. What this "theory" was I shall explain later and link it with *The Man Who Lived Underground*.

Some years ago a series of moving pictures—perhaps many of them are still being shown somewhere in the theatres of the nation today—came out of Hollywood depicting the adventures of an invisible man, or a man who had discovered a way of making himself invisible, or a scientist who had concocted a means of rendering objects or persons invisible. I mention these melodramatic movies because their influence, direct and indirect, found their way into *The Man Who Lived Underground*. Now, it happens that the idea of invisibility dates back in my life to the religious teachings of my childhood, for my grandmother's entire attitude toward life was based upon "the substance of things hoped for, and the evidence of things unseen"; and, in contrast, I always wanted to see and touch what I believed, or arrive at its reality through modes of deductive, inductive, or associational reasoning. My hostility toward my grandmother's religion did not keep its influence from registering upon my sensibilities during my adolescence, for my critical faculties were not developed enough for me to fight it off completely.

Whenever movies depicting the antics of invisible men were being shown, I could not rest until I had gone to see them, yet not knowing why they fascinated me so. I did not suspect that I was really enjoying the fulfillment of many of the folktales, fables, stories, and interpretations of life told me by my mother and grandmother when I was a child. It was not until these movies had made me think and feel so intensely that the relationship—the associational linkage between the two widely separated things—made itself manifest in me. Then I discovered that during all of my childhood I had lived among people who believed in invisible men, who believed that God, though invisible, actively regulated the most concrete and commonplace happenings of life. I think that it is but natural that I should have become excited over the question of how it would feel to stand outside of life and look at life.

At one period of my adolescence I thought that the twinkling of the stars was caused by the flight of angels to and fro in Heaven. (You see, I thought that stars were but ventilation holes in the floor of Heaven and their brightness was the gleam of an eternal sun that shone night and day!) Why should not the idea of invisibility intrigue me inasmuch as almost every day in my childhood someone reminded me solemnly that invisible angels were guarding my destiny? And the people who said this were willing and anxious to leave this world—for dying was but a transfiguration!—and go to Heaven where they could look down upon the sorrows of the life of this world without being a part of it, without being subject to its penalties and limitations.

I shall now relate another experience from my childhood to show how such things can be instilled into a child and yet when that child manifests it in his conduct it will be rejected by the parent who did not think that the child would dare carry out their teachings in a literal manner. I was living in Jackson, Mississippi, when the Leopold and Loeb trial was a

subject of national discussion. I remember one summer afternoon when the entire family had gathered upon the front
porch—the older people sat on the porch and the children sat
on the steps—and were listening intently to my uncle who was
reading a newspaper account of the trial, and of how Leopold
and Loeb were so brilliant that, though but nineteen years,
they had learned to speak German, French, and Spanish.
Suddenly I, a Negro boy who had not in all my life ever heard
any language spoken but English, had a strange desire to *hear*
other languages, and especially *English*!

"Uncle, how does German sound?" I asked.

"Why, I imagine it sounds to a German just like English
sounds to you," he explained.

"I wish I could forget English for a few minutes, just so I
could listen to it and hear how it sounds," I piped up brightly.

The array of elderly Negroes—my blood relatives on the
porch there—were struck dumb that summer afternoon. They
stared at me. Then my uncle leaned forward.

"That boy is coming to no good end," he said, shaking his
head. "Imagine someone saying that he wants to forget *his*
language so he can hear how it sounds!"

Yet it seemed that they could not realize that it was their
teaching me their religion, their encouraging me to live beyond the world, to be *in* the world but not *of* the world, that
had implanted the germ of such ideas in me. This is another
experience that gradually found its way, in a modified form,
into *The Man Who Lived Underground*. Years later anything of
this emotional complexion that ever rose in my experience
reminded me of those early experiences. It may be that those

events that create fear or enchantment in a young mind are the ones whose impressions last longest; it may be that the neural paths of response made in the young form the streets, tracks, and roadways over which the vehicles of later experiences run. . . . It may be that a man goes through life seeking, blindly and unconsciously, for the repetition of those dim webs of conditioning which he learned at an age when he could make no choice. . . . This, of course, is speculation.

Especially did Mark Twain's *What Is Man?* intrigue me by the manner in which Twain stood outside of human life and gazed at it; in reading that book my mind and feelings were swept back to the teachings and attitudes of my grandmother. I've often wondered just what kind of childhood conditioning must Mark Twain have undergone to have made his mind run so often into such channels. Though a white American, a mocker of religion, he, too, perhaps, must have caught some inkling of the tendency so widespread in the vast Mississippi Valley that made men and women stand aside and gaze with wistful, baffled eyes upon the riddle of their existence. In my reading of Twain my childhood experiences would return and make what I was reading seem *strangely familiar.* . . . (The recurring motif of the *strangely familiar* that runs through *The Man Who Lived Underground* was based entirely upon my memories of those years of reading and living. I've often wondered if there is a relationship between religion and crime, that is, what is the effect of the story of Christ's death and agony upon the cross upon children of five and six years of age. I've heard parents express horror at their children listening to crime stories on the radio; yet on Sunday mornings they never hesitate to send them off to Sunday school to hear the most horrific story of all. . . .)

This, I think, is about all I can account for of the ideas that went into *The Man Who Lived Underground* in terms of actual childhood memories; the rest of the concepts and materials were more deliberately arrived at; they came through thought, reading, and talking with others. I think that the best way to begin is to go back and link one of the experiences I've already described with some of the "theories" I picked up in northern cities. The first and most powerful occurred when my grandmother was still alive and was living with me in Chicago. At that time, of course, I had all but swept my life clean—at least to my satisfaction—of the religious influences of my grandmother; indeed, I had gone so far as to embrace a concept of life totally opposed to that held by her. Yet one day I went to the library and got a book that miraculously linked my grandmother's life to my own in a most startling manner; a book that had the strange power of rousing sleeping memories and bridging gulfs between peaks of forgetfulness, making many separate memories one vast web of recollection.

The book was Gertrude Stein's *Three Lives*. How did I, a Mississippi-born, grammar-school graduate, Negro boy come in contact with such a highly mannered book of this sort? Well, I heard of it through reading a newspaper account of a very funny woman who was always talking about "a rose is a rose is a rose" and who smoked a rare form of dope in a pipe three feet long while reclining upon a satin couch. I was solemnly assured by the man who had written the account in the newspaper that this woman was "stone crazy"; but, in his condemnation of her, he made one exception: He said that Stein's story of a Negro girl, "Melanctha," was really a good story, even though slightly screwy.

Being curious to read anything about Negroes—or maybe because I was unemployed most of the time and idleness is a form of curiosity!—I went to the library and got *Three Lives* and brought it directly into the home where my grandmother lived. Two more utterly dissimilar things, on the face of it, I imagine, never were brought into closer juxtaposition. (At this time my grandmother would not dare molest my books; I was helping to pay the bills in those days. The northern environment awed and baffled her and my ability to earn a few dollars had given me a new value in her eyes. It may be that she weighed the difference between having rent paid and the moral satisfaction of burning books she hated and decided in favor of rent! The North had undermined her mores to that extent. . . .) I took the book into my room and commenced to read "Melanctha" and, suddenly, the vague, foolish wish I'd made in the sunshine of a summer afternoon in Mississippi, on the steps of my home with the older folks sitting on the porch, was gratified. While turning the pages of "Melanctha" I suddenly began to hear the *English* language for the first time in my life! And not only that, but I heard English as *Negroes* spoke it: simple, melodious, tolling, rolling, rough, infectious, subjective, laughing, cutting. . . . Words that I'd used every day but whose power I'd never suspected . . . Words which I'd known all of my life but which I'd never really heard . . . And not only the words, but the winding psychological patterns that lay back of them!

But more than that; suddenly I began to hear my grandmother speak for the first time in my life! I don't mean that she came to the door of my room while I was reading and spoke to me; she was in some other part of the house. What I mean is that while sitting there reading, my mind was swept back over the years to the days when I lived in Mississippi, to the thousands of times when I'd heard my grandmother speak to me and I began to hear the intonation of her voice, the rhythm of her simple, vivid sentences. In fact, that little linking of memory opened wide to me the language of my entire race. "Melanctha" was written in such a manner that I could actually stand outside of the English language and hear it . . .

Am I piling a too-heavy burden of interpretation upon this simple incident? No; in school I was made to study the English of England, not the English of my environment; for every word I used in daily speech, my school urged me to use others on the grounds of correct grammar. That kind of instruction may be all right for a man longing to be a school teacher, or a man aspiring to be a bank teller; but it is death to a man seeking to determine the nature of his experiences, for he is taught to shun the very things—words used by his closest friends!—that may open the door to the vast world of feeling existing about him.

There is a personally poignant note to be added here; after having read "Melanctha," I began to engage my grandmother in long conversations merely to hear her express herself, in order that I could revel in the way she talked, the way that "Melanctha" had enabled me to understand. Then my grandmother died suddenly and I had to depend entirely upon my memory to reconstruct her innumerable conversations, speeches of endearment, admonishments, longing, horror, anger, fear, threats, exhortations . . .

I shall add another queer experience. In a leading labor journal—sometime after this—I came across a violent attack upon the prose of Stein, an attack that branded her the apogee of all that was degenerate in English and American literature. I was puzzled. Because I had admired how she wrote, I felt condemned too. Who was right? The labor critic or my feelings? How was it possible that I had discovered Negro speech in reading this strange woman's strange books? Then, because I lived in far off Chicago, because I was dumb and ignorant, because I was foolish enough to think that my reactions were as valid as those of a "critic," because I belonged to no literary school, I decided upon a simple, direct, naïve course of action to determine who was right and who was wrong. I took *Three Lives* and gathered together a group of illiterate, class-conscious Negro workers and told them to sit and listen. I read "Melanctha" to them in a dim basement room on Chicago's South Side and there were such wild howls of delight, such expressions of recognition, that I could barely finish. I was stopped many times by men who proceeded to improvise upon Melanctha's way of talking and thinking. They swore that they had met such girls, and I cannot mention what they thought was wrong with Melanctha and how they said they would go about curing her. . . . My feelings were satisfied.

The next experience that opened up a whole array of subject matter to me—subject matter which I've mentioned already: The manner in which Negro blues songs juxtapose unrelated images—was the advent of surrealism on the American scene. I know, of course, that to mention surrealism in terms of Negro life in America will strike some people like trying to mix oil and water; but the two things are not so widely separated as one might suppose at first glance. It seems that there has grown up in people's minds a concept of *just* what the Negro is, and anything that smacks of something which they do not want to associate with the Negro, for one reason or another, they will brand as alien. There is an unjustified but powerful tendency to regard the Negro as simple, unspoiled, childish, distantly removed from the debilitating experiences or art products of the city sophisticate, so says one school of the "friends" of the Negro. Therefore, they say, do not mix the Negro with any such thing as surrealism. There is no such connection, they assert, and if you insist that there is, then it exists only in your own mind, meaning, of course, the mind of the fellow who declares the contrary.

One might argue that if surrealism, product of decadent Paris, is degenerate, then the Negro is degenerate, for there are many evidences of surrealism in the art of the American Negro. This, of course, is a blind alley and gets one nowhere. Negroes are not degenerate and neither is surrealism, Dalí's crazy antics to the contrary.

Surrealism is a manner of looking at the world, a way of feeling and thinking, a method of discovering relationships between things; it is a phase of the creative process. And in folk art, where evidences of it are strong, it need not be called surrealism at all, if the word is objectionable. The Negroes of Mississippi, Texas, Arkansas have never heard, perhaps, of surrealism; but that does not negate the strong surrealistic structure and function of many of their folk utterances in song and music. Therefore, if the meaning of surrealism can be wrenched from its association—that is, in people's *minds*—with "crazy Paris artists" and viewed as a *way of seeing relations* between things, perhaps the idea of degeneracy can be dispensed with, to the greater understanding of the function of the creative process.

As I see it, surrealism is not an art form or an art movement manufactured by individuals or sets of individuals; I believe it makes its appearance when certain social relations are manifested in society, social relations that separate men from the context of productive process in a vital sense. This may occur at the "top" of the social structure as well as at the "bottom," among the sons of the rich as well as among the sons of the poor. One of the marked characteristics of surrealism is a certain *psychological distance*—even when it deals with realistic subject matter—from the functional meanings of society. This distance may derive from excessive wealth which enables one to live psychologically distant from the realistic processes of society, or it may come through an *enforced severance*—through unemployment, oppression, etc.—from the functional meanings of society. How does this psychological distance manifest itself? Primarily, I think, in the oblique vision which finds relations between objects which are seemingly unrelated. Hence, though qualitatively different, there are elements of surrealism in "Dink's Blues" that link them with the wild canvasses of Dalí. . . .

This obliqueness of vision is different in its origin on both planes and the difference is a matter of consciousness: The blues possess unconscious elements of surrealism and Dalí's canvasses are highly conscious and intentional, and both elements are *distant* from the habits of thought and feeling of the man who lives his life in terms of bread-and-butter. Here, I think, we have the answer to the question about why Stravinsky is attracted to jazz music; he should be, for there is a definite kinship.

Negro jazz music has been called time and again by many critics the greatest surrealistic music ever heard in human history. Of course, I doubt if Louis Armstrong, Duke Ellington, or Count Basie ever talk of surrealism in terms of Freud's theory of the dream structure and function. But, as many critics have pointed out, jazz music proceeds on the basis of a steady beat in the bass and then there is an endless series of improvised, tone-colored melodies carried on in terms of rhythm—sometimes as many as *five*—intense, moving to and fro between the keys, guided not by musical theory, but by the urge to express something *deeply felt*. Much of this music is created by men and women who do not even know how to read musical notes.

If one does not want to call this process surrealism, one need not do so; I see no particular advantage in arguing about names if the fundamental process is well understood. What I'm striving to do is drive home a function of a certain phase of the creative process, that is, the ability to take seemingly unrelated images and symbols and link them together into a meaningful whole. You have seen examples of surrealistic painting; you've heard examples of surrealism in jazz music;

and you've read examples of surrealism in, say, the tales of Poe. Over and above the element of distance, another outstanding trait of surrealism is its great intensity, its sustained dynamics. The most conspicuous example of this is to be found in jazz music with its continuous beat in the bass and the profuse improvisation of tense tonal-melody-rhythms.

Still another experience threads its way through *The Man Who Lived Underground* and, too, this new experience—or, I might say, the new ideas I came across which eventually became linked in my memory with my grandmother's religious disposition—was also linked with surrealism. In fact, I encountered the surrealistic theory of art at about the time I encountered the theory of psychoanalysis. Though I'm no exponent of the so-called Freudian view of personality, I do want to indicate the seeming relationship between the blues and jazz and swing, my grandmother's world view, surrealism, and Freud's description of the dream process.

At this late date I don't think that one need elaborate Freud's theory of the dream process; even high school students speak of displacement, condensation, inversion, substitution, over-determination, transference, and so forth. In varying degrees these same processes occur in many blues songs, in jazz music, and in much folk verse; if you should read the words to Bessie Smith's "Empty Bed Blues," you would find no logic or progression between the verses; they are merely a series of incidents of domestic discord and defeated love thrown seemingly carelessly together. But they have a relationship stitched through their inner structure, a testimony to reality seen through Negro eyes that look at life from a position of enforced severance. What takes place, therefore, is a seeming and relative confusing of values; there is displacement, intensity, transference, inversion, condensation, over-determination, and all of the other processes that go to make up the *strangely familiar* reality of a dream. All the details in blues songs have poured into them through sheer emotional intensity of the participants a degree of that overemphasis that lifts them out of their everyday context and exalts them to a plane of vividness that strikes one with wonderment.

Listening times without number to these expressions of folk utterance, they gradually stamped themselves upon my mind; the realization of them did not come in the order in which I've named them and my grasp of them was long and slow in the making. In fact, many of them did not occur to me until I was in the actual process of writing *The Man Who Lived Underground*.

I might pause to speculate just why it is that blues and jazz and swing music possess this intensity, why such an ordering of materials produces such effects. I really don't know. One critic comments that it is because of its collective nature, that, in a blues song, the participants are never called upon to stop and discuss what makes their songs sad, or why there should be a constant beat in the bass. These songs were handed down through tradition and the singers and musicians simply take all of that for granted. Another critic claims that the strong beat in Negro blues and jazz music, the heavy, melancholy throb, stems from centuries of oppression. It may be, I don't know.

Anyway, it can be explained in other terms, terms of a

technical nature, which are more likely to be acceptable. The moment one takes, in an effort at expression, a terrible lot for granted, and then proceeds on the basis of that as one's basic mood, to improvise, one creates an intensity. And it is that kind of an intensity that I tried to get into *The Man Who Lived Underground*. The first pages of *The Man Who Lived Underground* deal with a nice, honest, Christian Negro boy walking along a street, going home to his wife who is about to give birth. He is picked up by the police, beaten, tortured, and charged with a horrible crime which he did not commit. This accusation served me functionally as the basis which I could take for granted. That is, the guilt theme served as the steady beat upon which I proceeded to improvise, as freely and recklessly as I wanted, all of the images and symbols that my mind could conceive. I had the feeling while writing that anything that happened to come into my mind would fit. No matter how seemingly alien the items were, I could push them into this new frame of mind and give them a meaning which they did not otherwise have.

The cardinal joy in such writing stems from the feeling of *freedom*! That, above all. Here, in *The Man Who Lived Underground*, for the first time in my writing, I could burrow into places of American life where I'd never gone before, and link that life organically with my basic theme; and not only link it, but link it in a way that carried—to my mind and feelings— an unmistakable relationship. All of this leads me to speak of another element in writing which may or may not be derived or linked with this basic Negro form, jazz. From my earliest attempts at writing I discovered that I was striving to get to a *certain point* in my story; what I mean is this: I'd start out to tell a story, but I'd know when that story really *started*. The story would start at that point when my character was *broken*. What does *broken* mean? Well, in a good story, I think, there comes a point where the character is rendered *fluid*, where, through a combination of events, he is lifted to a point of *tension* where the author can do *anything* with him, where everything fits. It is like a fast train starting out and as it goes along it picks up speed to the extent that it begins to suck all the little loose matter lying along the railroad track into the air; it is that point in a story where the character, hard put upon from within or without, forgets his habits, his backgrounds, his censor, his conditioning and, feeling free, acts with a latitude which he could not and did not possess in the narrow context of daily life. I feel that something of the same thing happens in a jazz song; when the beat establishes itself sufficiently, all kinds of surprise rhythms can be introduced. In fact, you expect them as you hear the music or read the story. Of course, you do not know what is coming next. That uncertainty about what is coming next is the *drama* of the thing. . . .

This is as close as I can come to explaining this. Maybe I can approach it from another way, a way which might shed more light than the one I've just used? In the progression of a story or a novel there seems to come a point—in the beginning or in the middle or in the end—where the story seems to float, where any or many developments can take place with perfect acceptance on the part of the audience. A certain *heat* is generated, like the blow of an acetylene torch melting metals and fusing them together into one.

The best examples I can give—even if they are poor—are from my own work. The whole of *12 Million Black Voices* takes for granted that the reader is with me. Having assumed that, I begin from the first word to *improvise*, selecting the materials that fit the basic beat of the work. In *Native Son* the *breaking* point came after Bigger committed his first murder; from that point on the story could have gone in any number of directions with ease. In "Big Boy Leaves Home" it occurs when the white woman accidentally stumbles upon the four naked, black boys in the swimming hole. In "Down By the Riverside" the flood forms the *breaking* point at the very outset. It opens in a fluid state with a hurried flashback over the recent past establishing the scene of danger and action. In "Long Black Song" the *breaking* point is in the beginning: the sexual restlessness of Sarah forms the pivot upon which the story can swing in any direction. In "Fire and Cloud" the *breaking* point comes near the end, when Reverend Taylor, after being beaten, is informed that his beating is but one of many. In "Bright and Morning Star" it comes when Aunt Sue realizes that she has unwittingly betrayed her comrades.

From the character's point of view this breaking, in my opinion, represents a point in life where the past falls away and the character must, in order to go on living, fling himself upon the face of the formless night and create a world, a *new* world, in which to live. To me—rightly or wrongly—the hallmark of good writing resides precisely in this sense of creating the *new*, the *freedom* and the *need* and the *desire* to create this new.

Obviously, such opportunities do not come often to us who

live in this slow, real, hard world of ours. Change comes slowly. But in art we may reap our share of change—in as real a sense as we get it in life—in a few hours. Why is this? Maybe it is to prepare us for changes when they come in life? Maybe it is to compensate? Maybe it is to simply exercise ourselves in enjoyment? I don't know and I don't think it's important to find an answer. We have the *freedom* to make of it what we *will*.

In *The Man Who Lived Underground* the spot where improvisation takes place is the sewer. Here, in the underground, Fred Daniels comes across a wide variety of images and symbols whose reality came entirely from the original false accusation of murder. Hence, what Fred Daniels sees underground is overdetermined; they are things seen through a magnifying glass of such strength that they take on new meaning. Little events which perhaps we all see each day take on an entirely different significance. Emotion charges them so that they glow red-hot and are fused with everything that happens in the world. Meanings slide together. Events are telescoped. What happens is this: The world is *attacked*, is *acted* upon by a personality.

I imagine primitive people must have devised some such scheme for their religious rituals. Maybe magic is not so far removed from our daily modern lives as we are prone to imagine. To a lesser and weaker degree the same thing happens at a prizefight, a baseball game, a political meeting. That which is understood, that which is taken for granted, is the tradition, the convention; the many little experiences of each individual are pooled and each person agrees to accept what the other brings as his own. Intensity is collective, even when it seemingly manifests itself in a lone personality. Tradition is a dream, and he who does not dream cannot feel his own past, and he who does not feel the past cannot feel the need for the future. A dream is tense and tension is the prelude to action.

Fred Daniels's roused and tense sensibilities register everything he sees in terms of a man about to make a decision. The decision he does make is determined by what he can *take for granted*. He goes directly to the police, who had branded him guilty, when he has seen his fill in the underground. Where else is there for him to go? The police have given him his meaningful life, such as it is, filled with horror. This is not surprising; my grandmother was a stickler for obeying all the laws she hated and condemned. Christ had His logic when obliquely, he confessed His Godship to authority. (To avoid looseness, I might add that had Fred Daniels been lucky enough to have had a different past, dream, and tradition, he would have acted differently.) The criminal who returns, in spite of himself, to the scene of his crime, the murderer, full of remorse, who goes to the police, is performing more than an overt act. He is *completing* a logical circle of feeling over which he, within the limits in which he lives, has no control. Man does not and cannot live alone, and if he tries to, he ceases to be a man. To return to that which first stamped upon one's sensibilities the meaningful patterns of value is as natural as a swimmer returning to the sandy, solid shore from which he took off in a dive. What shore any man returns to depends upon what he saw while swimming and the kind of shore from which he first took off. . . .

If dream is tradition, then ritual is waking sleep. Unfortunately, we in America have few real rituals. But in ritual each item of the past is an over-determined detail of the dream come alive. The emotions of past days are about to go, but a new emotion is poured out upon the old details to preserve the past. New goals and perspectives are powerful enough to transfer new meaning to the ritual details. In ritual past is never completely past; the present is never completely present; and the future does not exist alone like a curtain hung before the eyes. Instead, they are together, as one; tense, taut, filling the personality with *meaning*.

Hence the inevitable abstract quality—I have already mentioned before that there was a kind of abstract quality in my grandmother's life—in the way Fred Daniels ties things together, the way in which he ignores the personalities of people, the way he lumps them all into one huge crowd as candidates for eternity. The tunneling through walls, the holes bored through brick, are all for the purpose of allowing Fred Daniels to see the fragments of an environment; I selected his world for him, but he ties the items of this world together on the basis of his past conditioning. His crawling around in sewers might be linked to anyone's sense of groping through the days of one's life.

It was not at all difficult to arrange the structure in that manner; when one takes as much for granted as I did in the story, it seems that that kind of development flows freely of its own accord, with its own logic. One writes for times like that to come, when meaning and logic and image and symbol fuse organically. One knows with a certainty of feeling then that one is right, which no logical contriving with one's mind can give. I leave it for others to try to determine the value of the various images and symbols depicted; the order in which they came is something, too, which others may think of. I don't think anyone can ever really know, and if they should ever really know, I think they'll find that the search was not worthwhile. I don't think anything in the book has any value save within the limits of the overall concept which colored Fred Daniels's mind at that particular time. In other words, none of the images and symbols in *The Man Who Lived Underground* have any meaning in themselves; the meaning is only to be found in relation to other things, in relation to themselves as they appear in certain sequences; their total meaning represents the totality of all these symbols and images put together and their relationship to Fred Daniels and his fate.

Now to become more concrete in my descriptions. I've given as much of the general background as I can. Now I want to deal more with the actual process of the writing. (But first I think I should answer a question. One might ask: What then is the value of the story if the images and symbols in themselves have no meaning? Well, I think the meaning comes from our contemplating the entire *act* as one whole. There is a value in disclosing a human mind at work upon its destiny. Once we grasp Fred Daniels, we surely ought to know more about ourselves. The abstract dance of Fred Daniels is our dance on whatever plane we live, even though our decisions may differ from his as widely as chalk differs from cheese. It seems to me that a serious mind would want to know how some of the basic movements of *any* mind work, for in knowing, it will know how its own mind works.) I imagine it would

be wise right here to say one or two words before I start, so I will not be risking kickbacks. I do not espouse the cause of surrealism in art, or a Freudian interpretation of life, or the psychoanalytic structure of the dream. I'm merely trying to explain what I felt was happening to some of the material in *The Man Who Lived Underground* as I dealt with it. Surrealism, as an end in itself, has no value that interests me. It is only when the device is used to communicate that it interests me; and I think that it can be used to communicate; it has been used to communicate; and it will be used for purposes of artistic communication. So much for that.

One day this summer—while resting from a spell of writing on a long novel—I was reading a very cheap magazine that carries no creative writing in it at all. This magazine's purpose is to write up—in rough, reportorial style—actual crime in a straight, factual manner. (I think the history of crime in the United States is as much a part of our important history as any other phase of our lives; I know of no other act or group of actions that so gathers together the threads of personal, social, political life of the nation as crime! A crime may be likened to a sharp rent in the social cloth that reveals the texture of all the strands out of which our lives are woven.) Now I read an account—written by some newspaperman, I suppose—of how a white man, in Hollywood, California, in 1933 and 1934, lived underground, that is, dug his way beneath buildings from vacant space in the earth. At intervals he came out; but he prepared himself a rather comfortable room.

At once the idea struck me as possessing literary possibilities and I wrote a letter to Governor Olson of California—

because I was afraid to trust the account printed in the crime magazine—and asked that he send me a narrative report of the outline of this man's crime. By return mail the good governor sent me what I asked for and wished me luck if I wanted to use the material as the basis for a story. Meanwhile, I had turned the idea over and over in my mind and at least a dozen hidden memories began to grow up in me, clustering themselves around the idea of a man living underground. Several notions popped up in my mind: First, here was a way in which I felt that I could depict the religion of my grandmother. Finally, I felt that I had discovered a form that could do justice to the inner logic of her life. Here, I could push the all-too-well known Negro religious ritual into the background—I could with one blow knock off the trappings which had always branded it as funny—and get beyond the singing, the shouting, the moaning, the swooning, and the screaming sermons. Here, at last I need not fear that the outward guise would defeat what I wanted to do. I had often wondered, in thinking of my grandmother as a subject for fiction, if I could find a way of standing so far back from her life—details that linked her in the minds of the American reading public with the ludicrous aspect of primitive religion among southern Negroes—so that the details would fall away, so that the bold outlines that formed the true structure of her personality would fall into place; then and then only would one be able to see just what kind of a person she was.

So here, in the account of a crime committed by a white man, I suddenly saw where I could stand and look at my grandmother, where I could stand and point to her so that

others too might see what kind of a woman she was. Now, I'll say frankly, that I was not at all concerned with whether I wrote about a woman or a man. I imagine men and women react more or less alike to religious reality, or, if they possess a religious disposition, they react more or less alike to the world in which we live. What I was concerned with was extracting from my grandmother's religious personality a certain way of looking at the world and putting this "way of looking" into operation in an environment. So, at once, when I heard that a man had lived underground, it occurred to me that there was where I could make what made my "grandmother tick" live and breathe, be the character a man or a woman.

And, of course—the moment I thought of my grand-mother—the old invisible-man idea surged up; yes, I thought, here is where I can put a man *outside* of life and yet let him live *within* life, just as my grandmother had done. Then there came surging into my mind the political suggestion and con-cept of the underground. I thought that such an overtone, though not explicitly expressed, could form a certain theme. In Europe today the oppressed are fighting Hitler from the underground. Next, while brooding over the idea of that white man in California who lived beneath those buildings in Hollywood, I thought of the Promethean theme, the theme of a man paying for a certain illicit knowledge that he had gotten. I felt that it would be good to have my hero, when he went underground, discover some illicit knowledge. (Later, while in the actual process of writing, I found that I could make the whole theme of stolen knowledge ironical by hav-ing Fred Daniels discover knowledge whose utmost value he

would not exactly understand and on the basis of this contrive his death for a knowledge he possesses which is not of the highest value. Actually, Fred Daniels is not killed for the really dangerous knowledge he thinks he possesses, but for fear that he might betray secrets of the police department!) I remembered, too, that in the Promethean theme, we had in the death of the hero, at least, to be accurate, his punishment, an inverted assertion of the value of personality. It is only when something is worth dying for that life really becomes precious. I felt that to have my hero killed for this dubious knowledge he possessed would be a way of affirming his value; in short, I strove to make the basic theme, or ideology, of the book mean: an assertion of human hope and tenderness in a world drenched in brutality. The one thing that Fred Daniels accomplishes and exhibits is the *freedom of action*! As long as men have that right, the results of action will justify any attempts to save it, to protect it. Fred Daniels throws his life away, that is, when we see it from the outside; but from Fred Daniels's point of view he emerges from the underground to communicate what he has seen, and to give testimony to what one feels is a right worth dying for. Indeed, he has the right and scope of action to feel deeply enough and long enough so that what he feels and sees acts powerfully upon him and drives him to further action. (This, incidentally, is my form of patriotism: Give men and women enough of life to feel and live, then when the time arrives to fight for life, they will feel moved to go into action with no thought of death or the dangers of action.)

Still another strand that runs through the skein of the story,

suggested by overtones rather than through explicit speech, is the theme of general, individual, and personal rebellion which is taking place so constantly and often in the world today. Sometimes it goes under the name of "individual initiative," "rugged individualism," etc.

Still another possible theme intrigued me to no end, but in order to discuss it I must revert back now to Freudian psychology in order to explain it. Perhaps I can refer to two other things, also, to explain it. The seeming relationship of this man's feelings while in the underground to psychopathic personalities and to religion. As I wrote I drew upon these two concepts very heavily, for they seemed related to me. Perhaps their being regarded as alien to each other depends upon where they are found.

I'd like to go into detail here on this point, for in the writing of *The Man Who Lived Underground*, this kinship of insanity and religion intrigued me more, perhaps, than anything else. As I wrote page after page I was reminded of many psychiatric case histories of schizophrenic personalities. More and more, as the story progressed, I felt the writing to be a good emotional description of schizophrenia. The symptoms were unrolling as I wrote; I was not trying in any way to describe schizophrenia; it seemed that the very nature of Fred Daniels's situation made such descriptions flow from the materials. First, I noticed that Fred Daniels was withdrawn from the world; second, that he suffered a loss of contact with reality in a hard and sharp sense; third, that there was a gradual disintegration of his personality. Yet, while noticing this, I also noticed that this whole idea of a man withdrawing from the world had a striking similarity to the life of my grandmother, who, in her religious life, was certainly withdrawn from the world as much as anybody has ever been withdrawn from it, as much as anyone can live in this world and not have anything to do with it. And yet, here I was expressing all of this in what I hoped would be terms of art. I felt that there was or must be some relationship between psychiatry, religion, and art. Just what that relationship was or is, I don't know. I only report that I felt that such existed. Indeed, I can add another branch of human thought: philosophy. How these things link together is something I'll try to search for as the years roll by and maybe they'll form the subject of yet another book.

I'm not trying to say or suggest that every work of art proceeds out of some deficiency of personality, or out of some maladjusted personality, or out of the fact that a personality is trying to compensate for deficiencies; I think that the relationship is more subtle and obscure than that. Because of the lack of clarity on the part of most critics, scientists, or if you want to call them psychoanalysts, the failure to make that relationship clear has been the cause of a lot of confusion on the subject. For example, there are some books on psychology that intimate that anyone who expresses himself in art is to be counted among the maladjusted.

Now, my grandmother was surely a sane woman and I think that a judgment as to her sanity can be arrived at on the most academic basis, that is, she was adjusted to her environment, despite the fact that, in my interpretation of her religious personality, I know that she was withdrawn from the world. I do not think that one has to examine my grandmother's thought processes to arrive at the conclusion that she was sane; she lived a hard life and she coped with every problem that confronted her to the satisfaction of her neighbors, children, authorities, and other associates. She reared nine children, and, being sensible, she had a very modest aim in launching them into the world: keep them out of jail and keep them healthy. Well, that modest aim might seem to some like a very, very little thing to strive for, but in the harsh southern environment to raise nine Negro boys and girls and to keep them alive and out of jail in a land where they are challenged each and every day, is no easy accomplishment.

Yet my grandmother did all of these things without ever really understanding the world in which she lived; I'm quite certain that she did not know the relationship of one thing in her environment to another, that is, in an objective sense. The only relationships they had were wholly in terms of her attitude, an attitude borrowed from the pages of the Old Testament. She brought her meaning to the world, but the world never gave her any meanings that she could accept. That was the strange thing about my grandmother.

Yet, in many respects, a schizophrenic personality operates in very much the same way; it is withdrawn from the world; whatever meaning there is in the environment is brought there by its own temperament. The schizophrenic personality sees the world wholly in terms of its own feelings; it imagines things that do not exist; dangers are always lurking; it hears voices. My grandmother heard voices; she imagined things, too. I imagine that the reason no one ever called her crazy was that everyone who lived around her was acting more or less the same way. When I, in my childhood, told my grandmother that I could not see things or hear voices, I was branded the crazy one in the environment. Well, I survived that accusation. Perhaps, in fifty or a hundred years from now, someone may look back upon the environment in which I am now living and compare its tensions to some form of religion or psychopathic tendency. If so, okay; I hope they learn a lot, at least as much as I learned through studying the memories of my grandmother.

There is still another theme treated suggestively in the book, that is, the Christ legend; I've already mentioned Christ in the sense of a man returning to the sun of authority that first gave him eyes to see; but the theme I'm now speaking of is the brutal treatment of the superior man by his inferiors. I deliberately wove faint suggestions of this theme into the story in a rather ironic mood. I'm not insisting upon it or stressing it, but I did feel that Fred Daniels, when he emerged from the underground, was certainly talking a lot of good sense and yet in the context of the environment in which he spoke, he certainly was talking a lot of nonsense. For two thousand years the world has been killing people like Fred Daniels for saying what Fred Daniels was saying, perhaps for saying less guilty things than those Fred Daniels tried to say.

Still another theme, suggested in a rather muted way, is the problem of the Negro. After all, Fred Daniels is a Negro, and Negroes in America are accused and branded and treated as though they are guilty of something. They don't know what they've done to be treated so; all of which has made a lot of Negroes write a lot of impassioned books saying: "Look, here,

I ain't done nothing. Give me a break, for Christ's sake!" So much for that theme.

In writing *The Man Who Lived Underground* I tried to stress that phase of my grandmother's life, her religious life, that intrigued me above all else, that queer form of social distance coupled with an abstract love for everybody, the ability to hurl a skillet at me if she found me trying to read something and yet working herself to death to keep food in my stomach. I tried to express all of this in terms of Fred Daniels's complete and utter forgetfulness of his wife, a woman who meant everything to him when he was living a normal life. But the moment these ideas begin to well up in him, she is forgotten. Take it as an indictment of religion if you want to, but I think the theme has been hinted at before in Russian literature, especially in observations that Gorky made about the religious man who never wanted to aid the folks who lived next door but who wanted to help everybody at once and change everything.

The last theme—and some might say the most important: I don't know what value it has—I tried to weave into the book, or one might say the last angle I tried to weave into the book, stems from something purely personal. I shall not name any names nor give any dates or facts relating to geographical locations. I can only report that I know how it feels to be accused without cause, because once in my life I was accused without cause. And when you are a member of a minority group, or maybe I should put it this way, say, a member of a minority political party and you are suddenly and violently accused of holding notions you've never held, of having done something you've never dreamed of, I can tell you that it is one of the most agonizing, devastating, blasting, and brutal experiences conceivable. Fred Daniels's feeling of being accused without cause was woven out of my memories of having been accused without cause.

My memory of a period of two years in my life when many people looked at me from day to day and suspected me of having done something dreadful, having uttered dreadful political notions about certain things, taught me how to depict those feelings in *The Man Who Lived Underground*. There is something fascinating about how an innocent man reacts when a false accusation is launched against him. Looking back now upon my own reactions, remembering many people with whom I've talked who have had similar accusations launched against them, I can say that it reveals startling quirks of character and action. I have the feeling that the branding of an innocent has the knack of uncovering something about the very nature of life as a whole. If a man has committed a murder and you accuse him of such, I don't think he will generally act very violently. But if you accuse a man of something that he did not do, his behavior will be utterly unpredictable. It has the power of upsetting his entire way of life, coloring his feelings about people for a lifetime, and sowing the seeds of distrust so deep that they will grow and bear fruit for years afterwards.

I'd like to go back and quote one more experience from my childhood. No doubt this experience stands out above all others that happened to me during that period; it did such violence to my feelings that I merely have to remember it for all of the hot surges of shame to come back even at this date in full force, as fresh as they were at that time. While living in Jackson, Mississippi, the home in which I lived with my grandmother burned down and I and my mother and brother were shipped off to live with neighbors until the house could be repaired. My mother and brother and I were given a little room; my uncle and his children were given another room in which to sleep. Our room was next to the kitchen; my uncle's room was up near the front of the house. None of us had any money and we were hungry most of the time. I had a little job which brought in just enough money to keep us from starving. Whenever I'd go to the table, I'd go there hungry and it seemed to me that I'd leave hungrier than when I went. I'd rise from the table, looking longingly at what was left over; but I'd know that I should not ask for it, because it was not my share. I'd stoically rise and turn my head and leave the kitchen and try to forget about it.

I remember one evening I came home and was called into the kitchen and was fed. A lot of my little cousins were eating at the table and they were as hungry as I was. As usual I ate what was allotted me and then went into the front of the house. About nine o'clock that night, my mother and my uncle called me to the kitchen.

"Why did you do it?" my mother asked.

My eyes widened involuntarily.

"Why did I do what?" I asked.

"If you wanted to steal those biscuits, you didn't have to rip the screen wire off the cabinet," my mother said.

"Rip what screen?" I asked.

Holding me firmly by both arms, my mother and uncle took me to the cabinet.

"Look at that," my uncle said.

"Why did you do it?" my mother said.

Sure enough, the screen was ripped and the plate of biscuits had vanished.

"But I didn't do it," I protested, outraged.

"Everybody else says that they didn't do it, so you must have done it," my uncle said.

To this date I cannot actually describe the sensations that shot through me. I wanted to turn to my mother and place my arm about her and tell her that under no circumstances would I ever do such. But I could see by the hard light in her eyes that neither she nor anyone else would believe me. I was a pretty proud youngster; I would much rather have stolen from my boss man than to have stolen biscuits out of the kitchen safe. Never would I have ripped the screen on the safe. I told them over and over again that I did not do it and I spoke bitterly and in a highly emotional manner. I was not only trying to defend myself against the charge of stealing, but also against their basic conception of me that would allow them to accuse me. When a man is accused, he is already condemned in the minds of the people who launch the accusation, all the fine and fancy Bill of Rights to the contrary. It is a psychological law. No man will accuse another, rightly or wrongly, unless he has already cast that man beyond the pale of the just and honest and decent. While they were accusing me, I did not know that all of the children had already been thoroughly questioned and by a process of elimination, it was decided that I had stolen the biscuits. They imputed to me a hungry viciousness; they had decided that I was so contemptuous of them that I did not bother to open the cabinet and take the biscuits, but that I *ripped the screen* from the cabinet and took the biscuits.

I suppose that for the period of a month, arguments, bitter and violent, raged in the household because of those stolen biscuits. I don't know to this day who stole those biscuits. I would like to know. The only real thing I regret about the entire matter of the biscuits now is that I wished that I had stolen them. I remember as I walked about the household I could read the accusation in their eyes: You stole the biscuits. And the only defense I could put up was one that rendered me almost incoherent. I was not trying to defend myself so much against the charge of stealing biscuits, but against being pushed out from that warm circle of trust that exists in all families if they are families at all. As I look back upon it now, my whole conduct, my reaction to their accusations, must have convinced them that I was guilty.

For a long while the family regarded me in a special manner; my mother informed me sharply that from then on she was going to handle me with kid gloves. I was told that I was going to be watched. Well, the accusation upon which I built the emotional structure of *The Man Who Lived Underground* did not deal with biscuits. But it was something, if you see the relative sides of the two situations, almost as horrible as stealing biscuits. I believe that the man who has been accused of a crime he has not committed is the very person who cannot adequately defend himself. There is really no way in which he can convincingly defend himself. His shocked and outraged attitude toward the charges throws him into an emotional stew which makes him blind to what he is being accused of.

Every word he utters can be used against him, for he is trying not so much to refute the charges as he is trying to fight for his status as a human being, trying to keep his worth and value in the eyes of others, just because he is innocent. The first thing an innocent man feels when he is accused is that those who know him have let him down. Because he is innocent, he does not really know the terms of the accusation. In order to deal with the charges or accusation adequately, he must wrench his mind loose from his innocent way of thinking and begin thinking cunningly and craftily, begin to think in terms that he never dreamed of before, guilty terms.

When I see or hear a person offer a quick alibi for something he is supposed to have done, I at once have my suspicions that the man is guilty. Of course, all readers of detective stories know this. A man who shows up as a witness in court and says:

"I was thirty-six feet from the scene of the crime . . ."

He is asked:

"How do you know that it was thirty-six feet?"

The smart and cynical answer is:

"You cluck, I measured it because I thought you'd ask me."

Of course, the cynical answer does not negate the psychological indications that some guilt is there when a man can explain too much too readily, that is, when he is too innocent. You'd better search a too innocent man.

While writing *The Man Who Lived Underground* all of these ideas played in and out of each other; the basic concept of my grandmother and the feeling of guilt that she seemed to have in relation to life, her retirement from the world while living in the world. All of the images and symbols in the book are but improvisations upon this underlying, steady beat in the bass, just like a jazz player improvising when he is playing his trumpet. I did not ever know what image or symbol was coming next; my feelings guided me from one phrase to the other. In that sense one can say that *The Man Who Lived Underground* is a piece of jazz prose writing, that is, if you are not afraid of the word "jazz." I'm not.

Afterword

At age sixteen, I devoured the words of "The Man Who Lived Underground" in a sort of fever dream.

I cheered as Fred Daniels plastered his cave with dollar bills, hung up expensive rings and watches on the money-papered walls, and littered the dirt floor of his abode with diamonds, abandoning all notion of the capital value of these things in favor of a purely aesthetic, sensual one. They shone with fierce significance, illuminating how much unnecessary power we grant them over our lives.

I smiled with sympathy as he eavesdropped on the black church singers; like Daniels, I was at once drawn to them and frustrated by their apparent abdication of their own power.

And I felt dread as the messianic impulse took root within Daniels to return aboveground and tell the world of his discoveries, in a bid to set us free. He had shed the shackles imposed by society: so could we.

My awe for my grandfather's craft had reached its peak. In these pages, he had poetically distilled the rewarding and dangerous condition of Otherness (dwelling on the periphery of society), a theme at work in almost all of his writing, but represented here with unparalleled raw and flowing creativity.

Otherness. All members of oppressed minorities hold an innate understanding of it. The pain and violence of being othered can engender insights and freedoms of a kind not easily shared with those who have never left the bosom of comfortable belonging. Standing outside, looking in, the Other sees our relationship to the world in ways those not estranged from society simply cannot.

I did not think my appreciation for this story could grow further . . . until it did.

It would take me another thirty years to connect the dots between "The Man Who Lived Underground" and Plato's allegory of the cave, and so come to better understand why this story, more than any other of my grandfather's, had taken hold of me and not let go.

Plato's cave allegory tells us of a group of people who live in . . . a cave. They are shackled in such a way that they can gaze only at the wall at the back of the cave. A fire behind them projects shadows of puppets on the wall—shadows they mistake for reality, ignorant as they are of what is casting them.

Not much of a life, you might say. Perhaps one of the cave-dwellers agrees. He frees himself from his position in front of the wall, and realizes there is more to phenomena than mere shadows. Then, freed from the cave itself, this person beholds, with some pain, another light infinitely brighter than the fire of the cave: the blinding light of the sun, which illuminates a much wider world.

The disturbing power of Plato's allegory is revealed when

he explains to us what might become of such a person who then *returns* to the cave.

Just as he was initially blinded by the sunlight outside, when the man returns, he becomes blind within the darkness of the cave and cannot function well there. Seduced by his own broader horizons and deepened perspective, he feels compelled to bring his fellow cave-dwellers into the sunlight. The cave-dwellers see him blinded and less capable than before he left, and conclude that regardless of what he says, the man's experiences outside the cave have damaged him. They resist all efforts to be convinced of the benefits of a larger reality. It is, after all, literally beyond their power of imagination, and apparently has harmed the only person claiming to have seen it.

Plato made sure to note they might resist with lethal force, so as to remain within the cave, introducing a note of political status quo in the allegory.

Fred Daniels, fleeing the false accusations of a brutally indifferent, racist society, was knocked from his mundane orbit into a journey to the beyond. Daniels's chronicle is Plato's allegory *in reverse*. He escapes into the city sewers, where the broader horizons awaiting him are to be found *inside* a cave, rather than out.

In both the short story and the novel-length *The Man Who Lived Underground*, the stubborn constraints of societal patterning are not in the darkness of the cave. They permeate the bright world aboveground. Daniels lowers himself toward an inner sun, the radiance of which was unknown to him while he walked the streets above the sewers.

Have we surface dwellers been shackled within the context of light and freedom, and is it a painful, forced retreat from that desirable world and into a fecund obscurity that lets us start to see "surface life" for what it is?

Did Richard Wright think of Plato and his cave as he wrote *The Man Who Lived Underground*, and did he consciously invert the allegory? *The Dialogues of Plato* in two volumes were present in Wright's library prior to 1940.

If Wright did not hold Plato's cave in his mind as he wrote, this modern version of the allegory nonetheless speaks to the universality and timelessness of the archetypes at work in it. Plato might well be spellbound to read Daniels's modern exploration.

Wright's version of this archetypal journey drives home the perverse tendency for the shackles of perception to assert their dominance with arrogance. We resist change not only because it is unknown, but because we convince ourselves our world is already the best possible version of itself. It isn't just "better the devil you know": worse, it is that "the devil you know is *good*."

As Daniels feels his way through treacherous sewer tunnels toward the shadows of greater freedom, every citizen living out life aboveground in Wright's unnamed city no doubt considers himself or herself more free and better off than Daniels. And as readers, comparing the stench and darkness of the sewer with the world above, we would initially agree. Only if we can embrace the dreamlike experiences that unfurl belowground can we begin to appreciate that things are not so clear-cut.

Tacit in the age-old vision quest traditions from around the world—to which Plato's allegory bears resemblance—is the understanding that the vision seeker returns from this rite of passage enriched with insights and powers that society then benefits from. The seeker has been to places physical and metaphysical that no one else has been to, and this has tremendous value.

In *The Man Who Lived Underground*, there is no compatibility between Daniels's underground experiences and the aboveground world he returns to. Within the purely racist paradigm of Wright's own era, and of the world of his novel, Daniels is not even considered capable of any meaningful contribution to society to begin with, no matter what he might have tried to do with his life. At the outset of the narrative, he is dethroned from this already low point, relegated to even greater depths by being falsely branded a murderer. His descent from that abysmal point into the literal sewers should mark the death of any illusion that he might bring back to society something it could recognize as having worth.

Daniels's attempts to bring back his discoveries tell a compelling story of the excruciating waste of human potential within modern society. Daniels's mind is clearly broken by his ordeal. His Othering is a sacrificial rite, rather than one of becoming.

Daniels returns to the police officers bearing a gift he cannot articulate. One that they do not deserve and could not possibly understand. And these officers of the law are the very people who physically tortured him in a relentless pursuit to affirm their own false sense of superiority and aboveground reality. That reality requires that his brown skin envelops a life destined to serve their need of the moment. Should they need to mock and feel superior, he serves that purpose. Should they need a culprit for a murder, he is there. Should they need to erase evidence of their corrupt behavior toward him, his skin is there to be perforated with bullets.

Mortally wounded, Daniels falls back and away into the mysteries he wanted to share with them. The water carries him away to be "lost in the heart of the earth," among the elements of that same natural world that vision questers ventured into, but traditionally returned home from, to a hero's welcome.

Richard Wright put aside the novel-length *The Man Who Lived Underground* in 1942, the year in which his daughter Julia came into the world. She in turn gave birth to me another thirty-two years later. Wright was preoccupied with the kind of world he was bringing a child into, and the novel-length *The Man Who Lived Underground*, even more than the short story version, paints a picture of that world: one in which race is supremely deterministic, eclipsing notions of Truth and Justice.

On one level, it is this message for his descendants that captivated my mother, and then eventually me. After all, I was aware from a very young age that I owed a great debt to my grandfather: my growing up in Europe rather than the Deep South. He had done what few African Americans dared or could afford to do: he had left not only the South, but the North and its own brand of racism, for France. All with the express goal for his daughter to grow up with as much human dignity as possible.

Repulsed by the virulent Othering of Black Americans, he embraced a different Otherness found on distant shores. A better one, he hoped. As Daniels fled the aboveground world and its calculated cruelty, so did Richard Wright go into exile beyond the reach of Jim Crow and American bigotry.

My sixteen-year-old self felt that in his story of Fred Daniels, Wright was telling us, his children and grandchildren, what he had left behind by leaving America. What he had allowed us not to experience. I held no illusions about France's own version of racism, but I could only feel profound gratitude. In France, brown-skinned people faced low glass ceilings in terms of opportunities within society, and varying degrees of social exclusion within certain spheres, but physical violence was a more rare occurrence.

Now, at forty-six, after having ventured into the world myself in search of knowledge that can only be distilled by allowing oneself to drift and become vulnerable, I find it is Plato's cave that leaps out at me from the pages of *The Man Who Lived Underground*, and I am filled with an additional gratitude of a different kind. I was able to undertake journeys that did not break my mind, and to return with something of value, to a world that though still tone-deaf, may yet accept some of what I've carried back with me.

Malcolm Wright
December 1, 2020

Note on the Texts

UNTIL NOW readers have known Richard Wright's narrative about a fugitive who escapes into the city sewers as a short story. But two years before the story "The Man Who Lived Underground" was first published in Edwin Seaver's *Cross-Section: An Anthology of New American Writing* in 1944, and long before it appeared in his posthumous collection *Eight Men* (1961), Wright wrote a novel-length version of the narrative that Paul Reynolds, Wright's agent, submitted to Edward Aswell at Harper & Brothers. Harper declined *The Man Who Lived Underground*, and the novel, different from the short story in significant ways, has remained unpublished. This volume presents for the first time two previously unpublished works by Richard Wright: the novel-length *The Man Who Lived Underground* and an essay written to accompany it entitled "Memories of My Grandmother." A large amount of material pertaining to both works, including typescripts, notes, and correspondence, is held in the Richard Wright Papers at Yale University's Beinecke Rare Book and Manuscript Library. Other significant materials related to *The Man Who Lived Underground* are contained in the Selected Papers

of Harper & Brothers and the Sylvia Beach Papers at Prince-
ton University's Firestone Library. The texts established by
Library of America for *The Man Who Lived Underground* and
"Memories of My Grandmother" are discussed below.

Wright worked on *The Man Who Lived Underground* for
about nine months, from July 1941 to early spring 1942, shelv-
ing the novel-length version after the disappointment of
Harper's rejection. This was a busy, highly productive period
in the author's life, coming between his two most famous
books, *Native Son* (1940) and *Black Boy* (1945). He was also
wrapping up work on his photo-documentary *12 Million Black
Voices* (1941) and struggling with a long novel about Black domestic workers (the still-unpublished *Black Hope*) that Reynolds and Aswell were trying to coax from their star author.
Native Son had been a literary sensation, and the two men were
eager to capitalize on its success and Wright's new status as
America's leading Black author. On July 9, 1941, Aswell wrote
to Wright, reporting that "Mrs. Montgomery [at Harper] says
you telephoned yesterday to give your new address, and that
you also reported that you have finished the picture book and
are ready to get going again on the novel [*Black Hope*]. This is
grand news. I have been hoping all along that the new novel
could be ready in time to publish next spring." In a letter of
July 20, 1941, Wright reassured Aswell that "I am just about
finished with the text for the picture book, and I am already
toying with the beginning of the novel."

But Wright did not immediately resume work on *Black
Hope*. Instead, he put it aside, as he recounts in "Memories of
My Grandmother," to undertake another novel, inspired by

a bizarre story about a man who lived for more than a year in the sewers beneath Los Angeles, staging a series of burglaries from an underground bunker. "The Crime Hollywood Couldn't Believe," by Hal Fletcher, based on an account by Lieutenant C. W. Gains of the Los Angeles Police Department, appeared in the August 1941 issue of *True Detective* magazine. This crime story provided the kernel of the novel, which grew and became connected in Wright's mind with an amalgam of different elements from his own life—his maternal grandmother's religious disposition and understanding of the world, his fascination with the Universal Pictures Invisible Man films, and his interest in surrealism and Negro folk art. This transformation of experience into art is the subject of "Memories of My Grandmother."

The Man Who Lived Underground seemed to write itself after Richard and Ellen Wright moved in July 1941 from Harlem to 11 Revere Place in Brooklyn. The couple had married four months earlier and Ellen was now expecting. "Ellen and Dick have a charming, secluded place," Arna Bontemps reported to Langston Hughes in a letter of November 4, 1941. "Dick has a new dictaphone and all the trimmings, and is he going to town? Knocked out his new novel about religious life among Negroes in a couple of months. Written at white heat, as they say, 'The Man Who Lived Underground.'" On December 12, 1941, Paul Reynolds submitted the novel to Harper, explaining to Frederica Montgomery, "Here is the new novel by Richard Wright entitled THE MAN WHO LIVED UNDERGOUND which I spoke to Mr. Aswell about this morning." The "new novel" was not the one Aswell was expecting. But Wright was very keen on *The Man Who Lived Underground*. After sending the typescript to Reynolds in December, he wrote to thank him for his efforts, remarking that it was "the first time I've really tried to step beyond the straight black-white stuff." In "Memories of My Grandmother," written just before or after the novel was submitted to Harper, Wright states—speaking now to his imagined readers—that "I have never written anything in my life that stemmed more from sheer inspiration . . . than *The Man Who Lived Underground*." What happened next is not entirely clear, but evidently neither Reynolds nor Aswell shared the author's enthusiasm.

Why the novel was declined remains a matter of speculation. Some clues are provided by the written comments that accompany a copy of the typescript submitted to Harper, which is held at the Beinecke Rare Book and Manuscript Library. These comments, on 118 individual slips, seem to have been made by two readers, one of them likely Paul Reynolds. The other appears to be Kerker Quinn, a faculty member at the University of Illinois and the editor of the small literary magazine *Accent*. Both readers found the novel an uneasy mixture of realism and allegory, and Quinn in particular thought the extended depiction of police brutality against a black man in the early chapters "unbearable." Did Harper fear the novel would be too shocking for contemporary white readers, who might not wish to be reminded of the history of violence against Black Americans? Wright's biographer Hazel Rowley suggests this is the case when she argues the novel was rejected because it "portrayed all too clearly the arbitrary 'justice' of the world at a time in which publishers were looking

for more rousing stories." It is also probable that Reynolds
and Aswell preferred to see *Black Hope* rather than *The Man
Who Lived Underground* published as the follow-up to Wright's
best-selling novel. Like *Native Son*, *Black Hope* was a work of
literary naturalism. What would Wright's readers make of his
short allegorical novel? In any case, Harper rejected it, and,
with renewed solicitations from Aswell, Wright turned back
to *Black Hope*. Two short excerpts from *The Man Who Lived
Underground* appeared in Kerker Quinn's *Accent* (Spring 1942),
prompting a note of warm congratulations from Ralph Elli-
son to Quinn. Nothing more of Wright's narrative was published until two years later, in April 1944, when Edwin Seaver
included a short story version in *Cross-Section: An Anthology
of New American Writing*. The differences between the novel
and story are substantial. To create the story, Wright cut the
entirety of the first part of the novel (the aboveground chapters, including the encounters with the police), compressed
the second part (the underground chapters), and altered the
apocalyptic ending in part three (reemergence into the aboveground). The story is less than half the length of the novel.
Before its appearance in *Eight Men* in 1961, "The Man Who
Lived Underground" was reprinted three times, including
once in the anthology *Short Stories of 1945*, edited by Bennett
Cerf.

———

A half dozen typescripts of the novel-length version of
Wright's narrative survive. The text presented here is based
on the ribbon and carbon copies of the last complete typescript of the novel, both of which contain Wright's extensive

handwritten corrections and revisions. Chronologically, this typescript immediately follows the one that Wright gave to Reynolds for submission to Harper in December 1941—and then emended in the late winter or early spring of 1942, responding to the many suggestions made by his readers. Either Wright or a typist then prepared a new typescript of 199 numbered pages, reflecting all his changes up to that point. The ribbon copy is housed at the Beinecke Rare Book and Manuscript Library, the carbon copy at the Firestone Library in the Sylvia Beach Papers. Wright made emendations to the first half of his typescript (pp. 1–85) on the carbon, then continued on the ribbon copy (pp. 85–199). Together the ribbon and carbon copies constitute the late working draft that is presented here.

Why he worked on two copies of the typescript is not known. Presumably he had them with him at different times and places, but other explanations are possible. In any case, the two sets of emendations are similar in character. Following suggestions made by the readers of the earlier typescript submitted to Harper, Wright worked hard to sharpen language, tighten episodes, and trim the narrator's overt psychologizing of his protagonist, Fred Daniels. He had already taken on board many of those comments as he worked over the earlier typescript, but he now went further. Additional fragments related to Wright's late working draft survive, but he did not complete another typescript.

To prepare a text of *The Man Who Lived Underground* that presents Wright's vision for the novel, all the surviving typescripts of the novel have been consulted; indeed, comparison has been made of all versions of the novel and story, published and unpublished, along with numerous fragments, to determine the nature and cause of variant readings, correct typographical errors, and interpret Wright's handwritten emendations. Wright never arrived at a final version of *The Man Who Lived Underground*, and it is not always possible to determine his intentions. Some revisions remained incomplete or provisional. Where it is uncertain whether Wright intended to include a passage or scene, or where the omission of material provisionally struck out by the author would cause a narrative gap requiring intrusive editorial intervention, the passage is retained. The textual notes found at loa .org/underground identify the most significant instances. On page 85 of the typescript, where Wright's handwritten emendations begin and end on the respective copies, his revisions overlap in a single paragraph. Here, this text follows the revisions made to the carbon copy at the Firestone Library, since the revisions on page 85 of the ribbon appear more provisional. There are a relatively small number of typed changes to the ribbon copy, typically correcting typographical errors. In those instances where the emendations occur in the first eighty-five pages and are at variance with the carbon, the text follows the carbon. There is a single sentence on the first page of the ribbon through which Wright made a light pencil mark. The significance of this mark is discussed in the online textual notes.

In matters of spelling and punctuation, obvious errors have been corrected, and in a few instances Wright's spelling has been emended for consistency. This text uses the modern closed-compound spelling of "someone" rather than the open-compound spelling "some one" (Wright was inconsistent on this point in his typescripts). This text consistently uses the spelling "hunh" rather than "huh," following Wright's usual spelling. Wright typically capitalized "mister" in his typescripts; however, the lowercase spelling is found in the final typescript of the short story version of his narrative (and in the text of the published story), and this text follows suit. In one other important instance, this text emends Wright's spelling in the typescripts: The closed-compound spelling "aboveground" is used here, as it is in the text of the published short story, where the closed-compound spelling is intended as a counterpoint to "underground." (So, for example, the text of the short story reads: "Emotionally he hovered between the world aboveground and the world underground.")

The provenance of the carbon copy merits comment. While living in Paris in 1946, Wright presented the carbon to Sylvia Beach as a gift—a gesture of friendship rather than an effort to publish the novel since by then Wright's narrative had a public life as a short story and Beach was no longer in the business of publishing books (Shakespeare and Company had closed its doors for good four years earlier during the German Occupation). This gift to one of the leading expatriate figures in Paris was also perhaps a self-acknowledgment of the artistic freedom and new life Wright was only beginning to imagine possible for himself in Paris (the Wrights would move to Europe permanently in 1947). Wright signed and dated the typescript on the title page, the first numbered page, and the concluding page: "Richard Wright December 9,

1946 Paris." A signed photograph of Wright, affixed to an un-numbered blank leaf, precedes the title page. The typescript is bound in leather with brown marbled-paper boards and a gilt-stamped spine that reads "R. Wright. The Man Who Lived Underground." It is unclear whether Beach or Wright had the typescript so lavishly bound, although Beach, as the former publisher of *Ulysses* and other important modern works, would have known the city's fine bookbinders. Either way, the careful preservation of the typescript underscores its significance.

Several references in "Memories of *My Grandmother*" indi-cate it was composed in the winter of 1941–42. There are two surviving typescript drafts at the Beinecke Rare Book and Manuscript Library. The earlier of these is a long typescript (sixty-nine pages) that contains heavy handwritten emenda-tions by the author. The later, partial typescript, which sur-vives in duplicate copies, ends abruptly approximately halfway through, but incorporates Wright's emendations and further changes up to that point. The text established by Library of America follows the later typescript to its end on page 26, and thereafter follows the earlier, emended typescript. Typo-graphical and other obvious errors as well as small inconsis-tences have been corrected; in a few minor instances the text has been edited for clarity. Readers looking for more detailed textual notes are encouraged to visit loa.org/underground.

About the Author

BORN IN 1908 near Roxie, Mississippi, Richard Wright won international renown for his powerful and visceral depictions of the Black experience. He is the author of seven novels, two collections of novellas and stories, and several works of nonfiction, as well as numerous influential articles, critical essays, and poems, and stands today as one of the greatest American writers of the twentieth century. Two of his works, his novel *Native Son* and his autobiography, *Black Boy*, are required reading in high schools and colleges across the nation. Wright lived throughout the United States, including Memphis, Chicago, and New York City. He became a French citizen in 1947 and settled in Paris, where he died in 1960.